Bob Becomes a Superhero

Bad Luck Bob

P.J Cruz

Thank you to all the chefs, cooks and at-home culinary masters that set out to make the world a more delicious place.

This is a work of fiction. Names, characters, business, events and incidents are the products of the author's imagination. Any resemblance to actual persons, living or dead, or actual events is purely coincidental.

Copyright © 2023 by Pj Cruz

All rights reserved.

No part of this book may be reproduced in any form or by any electronic or mechanical means, including information storage and retrieval systems, without written permission from the author, except for the use of brief quotations in a book review.

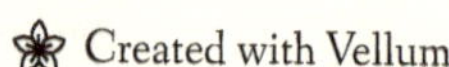 Created with Vellum

Chapter One

The alarm blared, its red LED lights telling him it was 8:00 a.m. Bob sighed and held his hand above the snooze button, contemplating whether he should press it. It was a tough decision. If he hit snooze once, he would hit it three more times and sleep for another thirty minutes, even if the alarm blared after nine. Extra sleep sounded heavenly, but he could also use those extra thirty minutes to work out for a bit longer or try to grab breakfast with Lila, his girlfriend, before she went to work. *Was she even awake?* He shut off the alarm.

He groggily reached out to his nightstand, only guiding himself with one half-opened eye. After knocking over his water bottle and watch, his hand grabbed the phone.

Bob had two texts. One was from Lila. She reminded him that she was going out of town for the next few days and wouldn't have cellphone service. She then wrote that she was excited about hanging out on Friday. Bob smiled and texted her back. *Sounds good. I can't wait either. I'll try to call you tonight to catch up. Lo...*He deleted the last two letters. Bob wouldn't say it over text for the first time.

It was tough dating a popular actress who traveled so much. They met back when Bob wanted to be an actor. It wasn't for him, but there were a couple of upsides. He met Lila, which obviously was the best one. The other upside was that the studio cast him as a character, despite being hired as an extra. Then, before the release a while ago, Lila was super busy redoing a lot of her parts. She said it was because the studio gave her more screen time. Then since she got more screen time, the studio made Bob more of a minor character. He didn't care though. They paid him a huge salary and attention from strangers made him nervous and sweaty.

After replying to Lila, he turned to the second text. It was from his buddy Charlie. *I was serious about what I said yesterday. I could really use your help. Don't tell Lila.* Bob stared at the text and remembered the context.

Yesterday, he and Charlie were at the Still Rivers yacht club. A mountain-sized man, Reginald Raghu, and the most distinguished-looking woman, Sarah Crafterson, had taken the stage at his parent's induction ceremony to their yacht club. They seemed nice enough, even if they sounded a little pretentious. Bob expect that though since they ran the club. However, Bob must've missed something because Charlie's eyes burned with hatred.

Bob rolled onto his back and stared at the popcorn ceiling. Charlie usually had a good head on his shoulders but was weird lately. Bob saw Charlie all the time growing up whenever he went to hang out with Ned, Charlie's little brother. Charlie usually joined in to play the big bad guy he and Ned had to take down together, but it was always playful and innocent. He even gave advice to Bob a few times about high school things like dates, or cars, or the teachers to pick. Then, a few months ago, Charlie made some terrible acting choices and got into some serious trouble with the movie studio where Bob worked for a day. After that, Lila was very antagonistic around Charlie. Even sitting at the same table as him during the ceremony yesterday was annoying to her. Bob caught her a few times eyeing him menacingly with a steak knife twirling between her fingers. She was also a little skeptical about Ned. Any time Bob asked for details, she just would say, "He betrayed the studio."

Bob sighed and let his arms flop onto the bed, so he looked like a starfish spread out under the bedcovers. People make mistakes. It wasn't like he threatened the entire world. He went back to texting. *What's up? Not hiding from Lila if I help.* A three-dot cloud appeared on the bottom of the texting screen and hovered there for a few seconds.

Then Charlie wrote back. *Okay. I'll pick you up after work.*

Bob let out a sigh of relief since he wouldn't have to clean up the wooden floors and beige walls of his worn-out studio apartment. His bed was pressed into the far corner, next to a window overlooking the city. Going along the window was his kitchen and kitchen table, both of which were tucked into the other opposite corner. The bathroom was on the other side of the apartment by the front door. In between the door and the window was where he kept his weights and where the TV-facing couch sat. Lila helped spruce up the place and arrange things, so his apartment wasn't as chaotic as it was when he was single. That included getting him a coffee table and rug that made it comfier, especially in the winter, to avoid the cold floor. Lila even put little sliders on the legs, so it was easier to move when they sparred with each other. She needed to do it for work, and Bob thought it was a unique couple's activity. She got a super determined look in her eyes once her gloves went on. It was just another quirk of hers he adored.

Bob sat up, rubbed his eyes, and got ready for work. As he brushed his teeth, he went over to his weight rack and did some quick bicep curls, switching his teeth-brushing hand after each set, so it was an even workout. Then Bob did some squats as he made toast. He followed that up with reading a textbook about being a manager in the retail industry as he ate breakfast.

The text was devoid of joy but very clear and logical. After reading a chapter, he slammed the book shut with a huff and slid it back to the center of the table. He could hear Lila's voice in the back of his head, reminding him to keep reading and that it would be worth it.

"What's the worst that happens? You don't like it? Quit and try something else," she said.

That was the issue though. He really didn't like it, but it was a direction. He tried acting but didn't like it. He had no idea what he wanted to do with his life. He thought about "finding himself" for a bit, but his friend Moni got in his head. She warned him.

"You have to go for it. You're literally dating a movie star who is smoking hot! You think she's gonna stick with some aimless guy? Bob, she's crazy about you, but I don't like those odds. She's not shallow or anything, but you got to do *something*."

Bob wrapped up things around the apartment then headed to work. On the way, he stopped by his favorite bodega.

The bodega door opened with the familiar bell ringing.

"Ay!" the man behind the counter said with a huge smile and raised arms.

"How's it going, Sergio?" Bob said with a wave, heading past the counter to grab snacks before placing his order.

Sergio was a heavyset man with messy black hair tucked underneath his hair net, a goatee, and an absurd amount of chest hair poking out from underneath his shirt and apron. Bob was convinced Sergio had superpowers because the man was always tan, even in the late winter.

"It's good! It's good. Maria is doing her, eh, SATs?" Sergio said, uncomfortable at the mention of the test.

"Oh, dang! That's awesome for her," Bob said as he walked down the snack aisles. "Any idea where she wants to go yet?"

The store was small, only five shoulder-high aisles and a wall of fridges opposite the window-wall facing the street side. Every inch of the store had the aroma of whatever Sergio was making. He cooked all the beef, pork, and chicken himself. The warm smell of cooked meats and the rich spices made Bob a happy customer. He headed back to the counter after grabbing a bag of chips. There was a different kind of clutter every time Bob came into the store. It was mostly gossip or home décor magazines, those tiny chocolates your grandparents got you (but no one ever ate) breath mints, and a few books. Bob perused.

A complete history of the greatest generation by Rich Penny.

Why kids are lazy and not as good as we are? by Bethany Chestington.

2,000 simple steps to a better life by Nathan Raghu.

Bob wondered if that last one was related to Reginald Raghu, who seemed like the kind of person with a lot of connections.

"No idea yet," Sergio said. "She says she wants to stay around here. I don't know why. Here sucks. Go to Miami!" He kissed his fingers. "It's warm. You don't shovel. You don't pay taxes. Moment she graduates, I sell and move to Florida. The weather, the music." He did some quick salsa steps to imaginary music in his head.

Bob chuckled. "You still have to pay taxes."

"No. It's legit! I swear."

"Uh. Huh. I had some friends who went to school down in Florida. It wasn't Miami, but they liked it well enough."

"I keep that in mind! The usual?"

"Yes, please."

"And how's the girlfriend? Lila? You know, I see her come by more and more. Knows your favorite order, she tips, has good conversation, very pretty. You are lucky!"

Bob chuckled. "She's amazing. She had to go on a work trip this week, but she'll be back on Friday. I actually got her a little something. I'll have her show it to you next time she's in."

"Ay! Bob, this is great. A good woman, like a Lila or like my Esperanza, there is nothing better."

With that, Sergio vanished into the back and the salsa music started up as he crafted Bob his favorite sandwich. A chicken parmesan sandwich with melted fresh mozzarella, and extra tomato sauce that Sergio made himself. Bob smiled as heard the fryer oil roar to life as Sergio dropped in the breaded chicken breast. His knife chopped up the basil and sliced the mozzarella to the beat of the song. Sergio was a musician of culinary notes, and Bob was his favorite listener. Soon after the music turned down, Sergio came back to the counter to ring up the sandwich. He looked a little distracted.

"That was fast," Bob said, pulling out his wallet. Bob

had ordered the sandwich at least seventy times and the timing was always the same. It felt like Sergio skipped a step. Bob noticed that there was a small squeeze bottle next to his sandwich. It was not larger than a glue stick and opened at the bottom with a "click-to-seal" nozzle. The label read *YummaGool Tomato Sauce* by Raghu Distribution, which was the Company run by Reginald.

"Hey, what's this?" Bob raised it up to Sergio, touching it sent a shiver down Bob's spine.

"Oh...I'm trying this new...tomato sauce," Sergio said, blatantly avoiding eye contact. All the energy from earlier was gone. "Saves me time, you know, and they say it tastes good."

"Yeah...that's cool. Do you...do you have any of yours? The stuff you make?"

"No!" Sergio slammed his fist on the counter but didn't look up.

"I'm sorry. I just really like what you make, you know? I'm...sure this is good, though."

Bob held it up for a closer look but only pinched the top like he had just picked up a full diaper. He dropped it along with his sandwich into his backpack. As Bob surveyed the store, he realized the YummaGool stuff replaced all the other tomato sauces on the shelves. There was even a squeeze bottle version that replaced the canned stuff Sergio sold.

"Bob, you be careful out there. The city...the city is changing," Sergio said. His voice was distant, like he could picture some great mountainous evil in his head. It wasn't like he was talking in the abstract. He shuffled things on the counter like someone pretending to be busy.

"You too. Tell Marie I said good luck and Esperanza I

said hi." Bob walked out with one last wave at a forlorn Sergio, who didn't stop staring shamefully at the floor.

Bob made his way to the bus stop. Central City was usually quiet in the mornings, at least in this part of town, which was more residential. Thin trees lined the uneven sidewalks every thirty feet. Parents and kids walked over to the subway to head to work or school. The locals stopped to chat with the business owners while they opened their stores for the day. He waved at a couple. The rest were busy or distracted, sort of how Sergio was right before he left.

Strangely, there were more food deliveries than what Bob was used to. He had been around for a while and recognized the usuals. The local baker would drop off bread loaves and bagels to the sandwich shops and grocery stores. Then, of course, there were the vans that brought the drinks or helped stock up stores with meat, cheese, or whatever else they were selling. It was a medley of names and trucks, but not this morning. Most of them were small, light-blue painters vans with the name *Raghu Distribution* painted on the side. Was that what Sergio warned him about? The change?

Before Bob could see who was behind the wheel, his bus rolled into view, and he chased after it. After such a strange morning, he appreciated the familiar feeling of almost missing his bus. Once he was on, he stared out the window. Even more *Raghu Distribution* vans covered the streets. All this business had to be how Reginald got to the top of the yacht club.

Chapter Two

Bob hopped off the bus and stared at the sign hanging above the door: Merlin's Warehouse. The storefront merely looked seven or eight feet tall from the outside. Inside, it was as tall as a cathedral. Bob asked the owner dozens of times how it was possible but never got a straight answer. He sighed and stepped in.

"Oh, there you are! I was just talking to Arty about you. He said you've been reading up and asking questions about being a manager!" said the owner in his sweet and wafty voice. He appeared from behind the long checkout counter to the left of the entrance. He was a tall old man with a shiny bald head, bushy eyebrows and a long beard that stretched halfway down to his chest. The owner wore an all-gray suit with a purple button-down shirt, the top button undone to show off his jungle of silver chest hair.

"Hey, Emrys. Ah, yeah. He's been great. Very detailed."

"Good. Good. So that's it? You're going for it?"

"I guess, if you know, it's something that's still open." He chuckled nervously.

"For a person like you! Of course! Of course! Only

"

serious people, though. I need mature employees who aren't afraid of a little challenge. The high stakes world of retail management is not for the faint of heart."

"Afraid? That's not me. I'm serious. I. Um. I totally—I want it."

"You can't even convince yourself! How do you think you're going to fool me? I'm a wizard after all. I've also seen how you handle the McCarthy's. Managers must be serious! They must be bold! You're a good kid, Bob. I just feel like you're holding out for something else. That's fine and all. This is retail. I'm not delusional.

"However, my managers must be committed!" Emrys patted Bob on the back and waved bye as he walked toward his office at the back of the store. "But of course, let me know when you're serious and aren't afraid of tough customers. Then, we can talk."

Bob bit his lip and looked back at the store. It still had a new furniture smell, even though they sold clothing. Bob never quite understood why, but that was just another quirk of "Merlin's Warehouse".

The store was a massive open space with clothes going as far as the eye could see and laid out by color, so it looked like a patchwork quilt. The mannequins around the store occasionally wore modern clothing, though some dressed as knights, wizards, witches, and medieval ladies. Bob strolled through the aisles to make sure everything was in the right spot. Everything. As usual, he had the store perfectly arranged. If that's all being a manager required, he would be perfect for the role. Unfortunately, that wasn't the case.

Things were usually quiet in the mornings, which was why he loved the shift. Plus, he liked the other people who worked mornings. There were only two downsides and they both just walked into the store. Bob dove into an aisle to hide, peering through some clothes to watch *them* enter.

Specifically, they were people from his acting days. One of them was a larger lady in her mid-50s, who "accidentally" stole his clothes and invited him to "private acting lessons" at her home with her husband. The other was her husband, who was just a strange guy. A few weeks ago, the husband had pulled out a sword from his pocket and plunged it into a mannequin after claiming it wasn't the actual sword in the stone.

Bob hated to admit it, but Emrys was right. Being a manager required handling confrontation and difficult customers. It wasn't something he went out of his way to deal with. He could act out a confrontation. It was a breeze because he knew it wasn't real. Before he acted in that movie with Charlie and Lila, when he worked tech, everyone was mellow, so there was nothing to confront. But here...in the world of retail...that's where the world tested a person's mettle. Bob tried interacting with the McCarthy's, but they always sent him running and asking for a manager. It happened his second day at the store and every time after that.

Luckily, one of Bob's coworkers, Lance, stepped in to help. Bob overheard the wife mention Bob's name, and he shivered. Lance lied to them.

"Oh, yes, Bob? He's not working today. But I'd be happy to help."

Bob thanked Lance in his mind and snuck off to another part of the store.

The rest of the morning flew by. He helped a few customers, checked the stock, and fixed some crudely positioned mannequins. Bored teenagers often came into the store to arrange the mannequins in inappropriate positions.

Right after he finished fixing the last one, it was time for lunch.

"Anything good?" Lance said as the two sat down in the breakroom. It was a beige carpeted square room with a kitchenette along the back wall and a round wooden table in the center. Another coworker, Percy, was napping on the couch.

"I...think?" Bob pulled out his chicken parmesan sandwich. He stared down into his backpack at the YummaGool sauce.

"You think? I thought you were getting Sergio's today. You swear by that guy."

"Normally, yeah. But he's apparently trying this new recipe." Bob pulled out the YummaGool and slid it toward Lance.

"What the hell is this?" Lance scrambled backward, knocking his seat to the floor.

"I've never seen it, but it was all over the store."

"Well...how does it taste?"

Bob cautiously unraveled his sandwich out of the parchment paper wrapping, waiting for the sauce's smell to slip out and infest his nostrils. He became so anxious he couldn't tell if he was imagining the smell of garbage or if that's what it actually smelled like. Sergio's seasonings and fry dulled the smell, but they were nothing but paper chains on an abomination. Bob looked at Lance, whose face had turned green. Even Percy had erupted from his sleep and stared in horror.

"Bob. Don't eat that," Percy said.

"I...I trust Sergio. It might not be as bad as it smells," Bob said.

"Please...Bob. Just take some of mine," Lance said.

"I'll be..."

Bob stared at the sandwich. The sauce wasn't even tomato red. The texture was smooth like ketchup. It stretched like Jell-O as Bob pressed the bread together and contracted when he released the pressure. He opened his mouth. The sauce got closer and closer to his taste buds, which screamed for Bob to stop. His hands brought it closer still. Bob forced his mouth to open wide for this first bite and clamp down on the edge of the sandwich.

"I can't!"

Bob tossed it onto the table. It crashed, but the sandwich kept its shape, held together by the YummaGool sauce.

Lance slid the other half of his sandwich to Bob, who reluctantly accepted it. Bob couldn't go back. Sergio might ask him what he thought, and Bob couldn't dream of crushing the man or lying to him. The best thing for both of them was to just not go back to the store. There was some fast-food joint or chain sandwich place he could go to. While he told himself it would be okay and that he would find another place for lunch, a single tear streamed down his cheek.

On the other side of town, two strangely dressed men peered into a bustling warehouse. They crouched on the roof of the building, staring down through fogged windows.

"You sure this is a good idea?" one said. He wore a purple jumpsuit that reached halfway down his thigh. Cork-colored body armor covered his torso and shins. His cork-colored helmet covered everything except for his mouth and beard. Cork horns shaped as mini wine bottles protruded out from his temples like a bull's horns. Plastic tubes grew out of the back of the costume and snaked around his arms like strands of red and white DNA. He spoke to the other person who wore a medieval knight's armor though each piece of the armor looked like culinary utensils, and he held a metal spatula as tall as he was.

"Of course it is. Don't be a chicken. We cased this place out last night. We know the exits, we know the rounds, and we know if we can delay them, it buys us more time."

"It's getting tough out there, Charlie. They're growing too fast."

"They're growing too fast and hurting too many people."

"We can't keep doing this alone."

"Yes, we can and we gotta do this. Now. We messed up bad with D.I.R.T. This is our redemption."

Ned nodded in agreement. Saying they messed up was a bit of an understatement for an evil organization set to throw the world into chaos, but that was behind them now. After everything flopped and they sobered up from the excitement of running an international organization, they realized how many people were hurt in the process. It also didn't help that their mom caught wind and gave them the scolding of a lifetime. She threatened them with community service. Though he was growing tired of his brother's dismissive attitude, Ned listened to his mom as did Charlie. They had each other's backs even when it lead they into dangerous situations.

It was just the two of them. Below was an entire warehouse of dangerous people. Ned and Charlie had combat training, likely more than anyone below. However, Ned wasn't sure if their training was enough to save an entire city from what was coming.

The warehouse was a long rectangular building with

dozens of steel columns forming lines throughout. Between the columns were tall racks, five tiers high and filled with packages of different shapes and sizes. People dressed in many outfit styles, ranging from bikers to hipsters, walked between the aisles or stood attentively. Toward the back, on the side of the building that faced the harbor, were two large open bay doors with trucks backing in. A few of the guards started shouting orders, and the workers unloaded the trucks, either bringing the packages to a spot on the racks or carrying them to ten small vans labeled "Raghu Distribution".

Charlie spoke up and pulled down his helmet's visor, which hid his face in shadow and only revealed two vengeful eyes.

"You ready, Ned?"

Ned readjusted his helmet so it was nice and secure. "For Central City."

He reached to his utility belt and pulled out a mini bottle of wine. After gingerly lifting the window, he tossed the bottle of wine down into the warehouse.

Boom! Wine sprayed in every direction and set off with such force that it knocked people over and the nearby racks wobbled. The warehouse workers shrieked and sprinted off to find cover. The guards started screaming out and running to get their weapons.

"They're back! Captain Utensil! King Grigio! Sound the alarm! Get the trucks out of here now!" one guard yelled.

The wine grenade then released a thick, hazy purple cloud. Ned and Charlie quickly rappelled down, landing with a thud and using the cloud as cover. Ned took a deep breath, appreciating the earthy aroma and the eerie quiet that had settled over the warehouse. It was always like this—

everyone waiting for the other side to act. As always, Ned struck first and struck hardest.

He burst from the cloud like a rabid bear at a nearby guard. His hand lashed at the guard's jaw and sent him crashing to the ground.

"Attack!" someone shouted.

Ned spun around to avoid a blow and squatted to dodge another. He lashed back up with an uppercut and dispatched another enemy. He glanced over to Charlie, who danced with his spatula, which spun so fast it sounded like a soft whistle before it made contact.

Thwack! A baseball bat crashed into a distracted Ned's chest. His armor absorbed most of the impact, but he still felt it, letting out a gasp of air. The blow was also powerful enough to send him tumbling into a crate. Ned launched himself behind the crate for cover, aimed his fist, and activated his wine blast.

From under his suit, his backpack kicked on, sounding like strong computer fans. Two shots of wine, one red and the other white, came out like an overpowered garden hose. They collided into his attacker's chest, and he stumbled backwards. Ned dashed forward, leaping off the crate and onto his attacker. The two crashed to the ground. Ned punched twice, and the man passed out. He then dashed over to the vans.

Ned flexed his fists, and three corkscrews emerged from his gauntlets and between his fingers.

"Stop him!" a thug shouted.

Ned took a knee and quickly fired the corkscrews into the vans' tires. He dodged another blow from a guard who swung a small iron pipe. Once he had a second, Ned hurled a block of cheese between two of the vans. As the cheese hit one van, it popped into a massive sticky web, which captured anyone unlucky enough to be nearby. The webs also held the vans in place. Ned hurled a couple more blocks until it trapped the remaining vans.

After appreciating his work, someone tackled Ned to the ground. They grappled and tumbled along the floor. Ned snuck an arm free and blasted the person with wine. He blasted the person again from his wine gun on the other arm. Then, Ned broke free. As the person recovered, Ned grabbed him by the slack of his clothing and hurled him into the racks, where some packages toppled over and trapped the person underneath. With the vans out of play, he could go wild.

Ned rushed to the next guard. Then the next. Then the next. He was unstoppable. Ned leapt over crates, swung through the racks, and took down anyone in his path. He did it with brute force or knocking things over onto a guard. It was only him and Charlie, but he moved about so quickly that the guards shouted that there had to be ten of them. Occasionally, one guard landed a hit, and Ned stumbled, but it only motivated him more. The attacks continued and continued until the warehouse slowly became quieter. Then there was one last whistle as Charlie landed a blow.

Ned sighed in relief as the last of Reginald's thugs toppled over.

"You okay, Captain Utensil?"

"Yeah." Charlie sounded equally out of breath. "I told you we'd be fine. See. You worry too much."

Ned bit his tongue to hold back his disagreement. Charlie was family, and sometimes you had to smother your feelings for family to work.

They gathered in the center of the warehouse. As he walked over, Ned could feel the adrenaline fading away and leaving his muscles hurting. Every step sent a sharp pain down his leg, at least until it got to the part of the leg that was totally numb. Blood dripped from cuts on his face and his nose into his mouth, over his lips, and onto the floor. His uniform boasted dozens of cuts and stains from different foods, sauces, and seasonings, likely from the packages he smashed during the fight.

Charlie was in equally terrible shape. His helmet had so many dents it looked like it was stuck on his head. Various projectiles like tire irons, knives, and chop sticks jutted out of his armor, and he walked around using his spatula as a cane.

"You should see the other guy," Charlie said, laughed, then coughed. The two collapsed to the floor, absolutely exhausted.

"We can't keep doing this." Ned shimmied up, so he was resting on a barrel of some inedible juice.

"There you go, worrying again. Plus, if we don't, this city falls. Everyone that is unlucky enough to cross paths with Reginald is done."

"You still have the medic gel back at HQ, right?"

Charlie nodded. He struggled to his feet and limped over to the vans that Ned had trapped earlier. The thugs trapped in the cheese web mostly had their mouths covered, so it muffled their screams. Charlie didn't react to them and peeked inside one van.

"Shit." He tossed a small container to Ned. It was roughly the size of a kid's crayon box and made of a plastic-film cardboard.

Ned caught and examined it. The packaging read, *Escargo to go.*

"They are insane. Who needs snails as a quick snack?" He tossed the box aside with pure revulsion, almost gagging just from touching the container.

"They covered everything in Italian and Chinese cuisine. Why not move to French? Reginald disgusts me."

Ned's body cried out as he stood and limped over to the other vans. Ned and Charlie peered into every one. Each discovery was worse than the last. Gum free bubble gum. Egg sandwiches with the consistency of Jell-O. Bagels and bread with the consistency of a tire. After reaching the last van, Ned turned to his brother.

"Things are about to get real bad, huh?"

"I'm afraid so. This is just one warehouse. Reginald has dozens of these places across the city."

"You said you had someone who could help us?"

"Just one..."

"I said no Bob! He's going to get hurt."

"What do you want me to say? We know he can fight. We know he's loyal."

"Great. What happens when this shit goes sideways?" Ned gestured toward the destroyed warehouse. This wasn't even the main one, which was on the other side of Central City at Sunside Piers. He remembered all the close calls he hadn't processed while his adrenaline was pumping. They had seen Bob fight before and he was good, but was that enough?

"*What happens when this shit goes sideways?*" Charlie mimicked. "Ugh, you sound like a baby. You hear how dumb you sound? Bob will be fine."

"Charlie, this is a bad idea."

"Look. We'll put the training wheels on him. No scouting solo. I'll hold little Bob's hand."

Ned nodded. Charlie was right. Bob was a good choice, and if he had training wheels, they could see if he was able to roll with them. The moment Bob was in danger, Ned would put the kibosh on it. Bob was one of his best friends and Ned wouldn't put his life in danger.

"Great—Oh wait, what time is it?"

"Little after 3."

"Crap! I gotta pick up Bob."

* * *

After finishing his lunch, Bob went about the rest of his day with his mind in a fog. The chicken parmesan sandwich was all he could think about. He focused on it so intently that he didn't remember what happened during his day. At the end of his shift, Bob felt like he had just woken up from a coma instead of working for four hours. Before he knew it, he was walking outside.

"Bob," a familiar voice said.

After gasping, Bob turned around to see Charlie, looking like he went nine rounds with some professional fighter. Charlie was taller than Bob and much more muscular, even though a baggy hoodie hid his build. He had short brown hair, the kind that never really lost its shape or needed to be brushed in the morning, and some facial stubble.

"Ah! Damn it, Charlie. You scared me," Bob said, catching his breath. "Nice car."

Charlie leaned against some black classic car with a boxy shape and four doors though it looked orange in the setting sun. The hood had a scoop in the center and a small panel on either side. It was hard to notice, but Bob saw more panels at random points on the sides of the vehicle that blended in seamlessly with the rest of the car.

"Thanks. You ready to go?"

"Go? Go where?"

Part of Bob was nervous that Charlie had lost his mind out of guilt for betraying their old movie studio and was going to kidnap him in some desperate attempt to fix his wrongs. The other part remembered that his mom tracked his phone location, and Lila had an uncanny skill at finding people. No one was kidnapping Bob without his two favorite women doing something about it.

"To show you what we're up against."

"We're up against? I haven't even agreed to help you."

"I know, but you will." Charlie paused and looked like he was mulling something over in his head. "How was your chicken parm? How was...the sauce?"

Bob gagged. "How do you know about that?"

"I know because Sergio's place isn't the only bodega that's been hurt. Now, if you ever want to eat real tomato sauce again and not that filth, you'll get in the car."

Time stopped as Bob relived the scene with Sergio this morning. YummaGool was everywhere, occupying every part of his sight and taste memories. So horrendous. Suddenly, the tubes of YummaGool sprouted eyes then legs and leaped off the shelves toward Bob. They chanted "eat us" as they approached Bob with a clear desire to eat him. Mouths grew over the *YummaGool* logo *and* gross Jell-O tongues licked what would be their lips. Then he remembered Sergio's warning. *Be careful.* It echoed as the Yumma-Gool monsters leaped at him and—

Bob snapped back to reality. While distracted, he had clenched his fist. His heart raced. It wasn't out of fear, though. His heart raced from adrenaline, the kind you didn't get from sports or playing an exciting video game. It was the adrenaline of a warrior wronged by an enemy that showed no remorse. The kind that required confrontation.

Before Bob even noticed, he sat in the passenger seat of Charlie's car.

"Drive," Bob said.

"Let's save our city," Charlie said. He reached forward and clicked a red button on the center of the dashboard. In the next second, the car whirled to life. The passenger side dashboard rotated and revealed a screen monitor listing different radio frequencies and the associated first responder agencies. The stereo flashed white, then turned into a deep and glowing red. It showed the normal media options and temperature controls, but it also showed choices for sonar, traffic control and "*Ask Julia*". Charlie's steering wheel twisted apart, so it looked like a long 'H' with curved outer handles. Small red buttons, the size of pincushions, rose out from the tops of the handles. Then the engine bellowed to life like Charlie had a colossal demon under the hood fighting to get out. The car screamed down the streets and into the twilight.

Charlie sailed through the congested streets with expert precision. Bob figured people would honk, but the engine and the *whoosh* sound of passing other cars drowned everything out. Even the traffic lights were on their side, turning green right as they approached the intersection. At first Bob thought it was magic, but each time they saw a light, the vehicle's console binged. *Change light?* Charlie clicked yes, and the light suddenly turned green. It seemed highly illegal, but they were already going three times the speed limit, so Bob sat quietly.

The entire time, Bob envisioned Sergio's defeated face as he dressed his masterpieces in squeeze-bottle tomato sauce.

"Bob," Charlie said, snatching Bob from his nightmare. "I'm really sorry for...what I did before. I hurt a lot of people. You believed in me back then and now. It really means a lot. I'm gonna need that from you again."

The car skidded as he ripped a left turn through an intersection, the tires screaming as people jumped out of the way.

Bob stared at his friend for a few moments, mainly trying to figure out what he meant by hurting a lot of people. All Charlie did was betray a movie studio and blow its budget. It wasn't the end-all be-all. Veritably, one of the studio actors, who was also one of the co-directors, told him it was borderline treason to betray the movie studio. Bob chalked it up to everyone being dramatic.

"Of course, dude," he said.

"Another bright side: Ned's helping me out with this. It'll be like a reunion. I can't remember the last time we all got together." The car ran over a curb and jumbled Bob and Charlie. Pedestrians rolled out of the way and showed their anger with hand gestures. No one got hurt, but Bob tensed up a little.

"Maybe you should slow down a bit," Bob said. "What's the rush?"

"I underestimated how long it would take to get you. If we take too long, your surprise might not look right," Charlie said.

Bob feigned a smile and tried to relax in the leather seat. He kept adjusting to find the most comfortable position, but he knew he'd never find it. The reckless driving made him too anxious and guilty. Bob did his best though and held onto the car's grab handle. The speed also roiled his stomach, which was normal. He often got motion sickness driving normally in the city, and this was a whole other beast.

The tall buildings and bright lights of the city faded

away as they crossed the east bridge. The bridge took them onto an empty freeway, with dense forests of leafless trees on both sides and a grassy median separating them.

"How are things going, by the way?" Charlie said, passing a car on the road.

"Fine, I guess." Bob's motion sickness had dulled since Charlie was no longer driving like a maniac in the city and the ride was smoother now. "Lila is great. Work has been tough, though."

"Tough? Aren't you in retail?"

"Yeah, but you know, customers can be difficult."

"Just tell them to piss off! That's what I do."

"Didn't you get fired from your last job?"

"Touché."

"But yeah, there's that, and my boss doesn't think I'm ready for a promotion. I mean, I kinda get it."

"Why's that? You're definitely qualified."

"I'm not good with confrontation."

They passed a few signs, too fast for Bob to read them, then the car slowed down.

"Yeah, I can see that. I may have gotten fired, but I never took attitude from a crappy customer," Charlie said with a snort.

Bob frowned. Charlie was right.

A few minutes later, Bob read an upcoming sign in his head that reflected the car's floodlights. *Condemned*. It was a bright green road sign, the kind that usually says what exit is coming up.

"Here's our stop," Charlie said softly, like he was turning onto his home street and the kids were sleeping in the back. Bob didn't feel the same. He reached into his pocket and started texting *SOS* to Lila. The moment things got sketchy, he would hit send.

"Uh...Where is here?" Bob said, his finger hovering over the send button in his pocket.

"Our home base."

The paved road stopped abruptly, and the car muddled over gravel. The tree branches interlocked above them and formed an ominous canopy, blotting out the moon. It was pure darkness all around them, only the car lights showing anything. If Charlie stopped the car, Bob couldn't see if anyone was approaching from the sides. He started sweating and his finger trembled. Adding to the fear was the idea of accidentally pressing send and Lila coming to save him from nothing. He was probably fine. Then his phone vibrated. Bob's heart stopped.

He pulled out his phone. Bob had hit send and now had a message from Lila. *Calling you now.* The phone vibrated repeatedly, and it said Lila was calling.

"Charlie, can you kill the engine? Lila is calling me," Bob said. Charlie slammed on the brakes, and the entire car lurched forward. Bob would've crashed into the dashboard, but his seatbelt yanked tight and held him in place.

"You're kidding me, you told her? Dude! Whatever, fine, answer," Charlie said. The car engine fell silent, and all the gadgets vanished, and it looked like a normal car again. Bob gave Charlie a raised eyebrow, then answered.

"Hey Lila, how's your trip going?" Bob said. He heard something like crashing waves in the background, then some popping noises.

"Fine. What are you bringing through the green glass door?" Lila said. Her voice went in and out like she had bad cell service.

"I'm bringing pools through the green glass door," Bob said. He was looking straight ahead but could feel the heat from Charlie's judgmental stare.

"Are you okay?" Lila said. There was the sound of someone yelling in pain, then getting swallowed up by the deep tumbling sound.

"Yeah, sorry. I thought I was in trouble—"

"Who are you with? Why?"

"I'm hanging with Charlie?"

"Really? Ugh, I...fine, whatever. He's your friend, just be"—there was more popping—"just be safe, okay. I miss you," Lila said.

"Miss you too, and you be safe too."

"I will!" Lila hung up.

Bob turned to Charlie, who looked sad.

"She's still mad at me for the whole movie debacle, huh?" he said.

"Yeah..."

"Dude, all I did was betray the...studio."

"Yeah, you betrayed the studio you both swore to serve. You really messed up, and it hasn't been that long."

"I'm trying. I'm trying to make it better."

"Sometimes that's all you can do. Do it and hope one day it helps."

Charlie turned on the car, and they continued the rest of the drive in silence.

The gravel road turned to dirt then stopped at a rickety wooden one-armed gate. The car slowly pressed forward, and they pushed the gate open. As they passed, it closed with a mechanical precision back to its original point.

On the other side of the gate was a dirt clearing, roughly the size of a little league baseball diamond and surrounded by trees. Straight ahead, where the batter would stand, was a boulder the size of a one-story house.

Charlie got out and made his way to the center. Bob did the same and saw there was a plastic picnic table in the middle of it, with a green barrel-sized trash can next to it. There were three glass jars with some Italian themed branding and filled with a red sauce. One had wreaths around a phony Italian sounding word, another had a man with a thick caterpillar mustache and the last had the largest tomato and a kid sitting on top of it. Behind the jars was a bowl of warm pasta.

"You wanted me to try jarred tomato sauce?" Bob said. He got closer and went to go pick up a jar, but Charlie grabbed his hand.

"This is a test," he said. "Watch me first. This way, you know the trick. The jar doesn't matter." He reached for one jar and tossed it into the trash. "It all belongs in the same spot."

Bob would always choose homemade sauce over a mass produced one. It still seemed like a waste just to prove a point...

Bob waited for the sound of the jar hitting the bottom of the can, but it sounded like the jar fell down a garbage chute, clinking against the walls as it made its way down. He peeped into the can, but it looked like the regular inside of the garbage can. Then he realized there wasn't a jar in it. It was empty. When he turned back to the table, there were three cans on the table again.

Charlie started walking toward the boulder, which left Bob confused for a moment. Then, as Charlie was halfway to the boulder, part of the stone shimmered, and a beam of light shone through in the shape of a door. Bob quickly jogged ahead as Charlie reached for a materialized door handle and said, "Hurry up. Your present is waiting."

Chapter Three

Bob cleared the door. The inside was mostly dark, so Bob couldn't see any walls or the ceiling like they were in the center of a massive, unlit cavern. However, dull lights illuminated enough to show steps made from metal grates. Thee steps lead down to a large, round, and smooth metal platform. The lounge area on the platform had a TV on one side and a dinner table on the other. The furniture was spread out enough to allow plenty of room to get around. Metal bridges stretched out from the platform, but shadows concealed whatever was at the end of the bridges.

"Julia, let's get cooking," Charlie said. Before Bob asked who Julia was, a feminine robotic voice, which sounded out of breath and slightly congested, echoed throughout the area.

"Welcome back, Chef Charlie," it said. Lights flicked on, revealing an area a lot larger than Bob expected. He could hear computer beeps and fans all around them. The formerly concealed bridges led to three other areas. Left and right bridges lead to closed vaults. The one straight ahead led to another platform with a jumbo-sized screen and an accompanying dashboard with a hundred buttons and switches. The screen blinked on, and Bob could see it partitioned itself between camera feeds, a radar of Central City and a window with a search bar.

"Charlie...what is all this?" Bob said. He grabbed onto the handrail along the stairs to keep his balance. Beyond the staircase and platforms was pitch black. He didn't want to know how deep everything was.

"This is my headquarters," Charlie said. He made his way to the left side vault. It was a massive gray steel box, suspended over the black below by metal chains, which vanished in the darkness above. The entrance was a heavy metal door with a wheel mechanism handle. He turned to Bob and smirked.

"This is where I start my nights. I suit up, then take Red back into the city to fight crime."

"Red being?"

"The car."

Bob bit his lip and nodded. "And that's safe? Shouldn't we leave that to like cops and stuff?"

"If cops handled it, I wouldn't have to. They're either too scared or don't know what's going on. So that's where I step in. Ned too, I guess."

Bob's stomach sank, and he began regretting coming along. Charlie continued.

"For too long, the city's restaurants have been plagued with pre-made tomato sauce. Normies have gotten used to the canned stuff, and it has led to restaurants getting bad reviews for the stuff they make. That was the dinner bell for criminals."

"You know you sound insane, right?"

"Insane? No. You know exactly what I'm talking about. Sergio, is it? He was hit a few nights ago. I tried to save him, but I was too late." Charlie sounded forlorn as he finished speaking and he stared down at the ground.

In the moments of silence, Bob's mind wandered back to the bite he almost took out of the sandwich. The aromatic and robust tomato sauce he had grown used to was now a bland and stale tomato sauce, which Bob believed didn't even have real tomatoes. The texture made it into a little more than a red, gummy soup, and it ruined the crispy texture of the fried breadcrumb underneath. Rage swelled in Bob's chest and extended out to his limbs, which screamed for him to act.

"That's why you want to stop Reginald. You think he's behind it," Bob said. Bob flashed back to his parent's yacht club induction ceremony and how each one of Reginald's monstrous steps shook the world. How many culinary dishes and dreams did he crush with one of those steps? Then there were Charlie's parting words that day—*he's the kingpin of it all.*

Charlie nodded and rested his hands on the spinning latch of the vault.

"I'm really sorry, Bob. I was stuck at Donny's a few blocks over. By the time I got to Sergio, they had already filled his shelves with...I don't even want to say it." Charlie spun the wheel, and a metal screech rang out. He heaved the door open, revealing a small room, about fifteen feet by fifteen feet, with stainless steel, stomach-high tables lining the wall. A weird mix of lab and kitchen equipment covered the tops of the tables. One table had test tubes and a colander. Another had a centrifuge spinning what Bob recognized as penne pasta. The rest was just as chaotic and messy, but a beeping took Bob's attention straight ahead. Along the wall opposite the entrance was an oven and a timer reading 0:00 in a blinking green font.

Charlie jogged forward, put on some oven mitts from a nearby table, and pulled out white-hot body armor. It looked like a thick morph suit for just his torso. The air trapped in the oven hissed as it escaped and turned the room into a humid desert. Bob thought it looked like the stuff he wore back when he was an actor. He stepped out of Charlie's way then took another step to avoid the heat coming off it. Charlie dunked it into a large bucket of water on the floor, and steam shot out of the top like a volcano, forming clouds on the ceiling.

"I should've timed this better, but everything looks okay," Charlie said. The steam dissipated and Charlie pulled the body gear out of the bucket with metal tongs and rested it on a clear spot on the table.

"Ta da!"

He held it up like a poster for Bob to see.

Once cooled, the body armor was a golden brown on the sides with a bold, tomato-red line down the middle, so it looked like a vertical sandwich. There were no pockets or pouches on the front, but the texture of the red fabric made the color almost look like it had red chunks built into it. A cartoonish emblem of a chicken parmesan sand-wich, the kind Bob ate almost every day for lunch and the kind that Sergio made him, sat boldly in the center of his chest.

Charlie said, "I wanted you to be empowered by the thing you were fighting for. It's going to be a tough fight, and we need strength wherever we can get it."

Bob pursed his lips. He knew he wasn't only fighting for Sergio. There were hundreds of shops or small restaurants that served delicious chicken parmesan sandwiches. This assault on quality ingredients and family traditions would affect them all. Bob and Charlie were the last lines of defense. He slipped off his lucky sweatshirt, laid it on the table, and then slipped the body armor on.

It fit his torso like a tailored glove. There was still a warmth coming off it, and the armor molded itself tighter to his body and his physique came through the front. "It fits," Bob said.

"Good. I got more to show you," Charlie said and headed to the other vault.

The second vault opened with the same heavy metal-grinding groan. Inside was vastly different yet just as impressive. On every wall, there were dozens of gadgets mounted, like display shoes at a retail store. Straight ahead was silver metal body armor, the kind a knight would wear, with an emblem of a spatula, ladle, and whisk crossing each other into a compass shape. The body armor had a matching armet, the lifting plate cut in the shape of a spatula, and pauldrons made of giant spoons connecting to the body armor torso. Below that were greaves with downward facing shingles and mixing bowl knee covers made of the same alloy as the body armor.

To the left was a mannequin covered with gear that matched his body armor. It had a golden-brown aramid fiber mask with a stripe of red going down the center where Bob's nose would be. Tight nylon red pants with a brown stripe aligned with his knee all the way to the attached footsie.

A mannequin stood along the right wall, but the gear was missing.

"Welcome," Charlie said, "to our armory. I am Captain Utensil, serving crime to justice. Defender of all kitchens and cuisine." He bowed. "After the whole movie thing went down, I convinced the studio to let me keep some of the technology we developed."

Bob recognized some of the gear from the movie he

made with Lila, Ned, and Charlie. He recognized the marinara grenades and wine guns. Everything else seemed a step removed from that. There were Wild West pistols with attached bulbs filled with marinara where the hammer would be, long thick spaghetti strings wrapped around like rope and throwing stars that looked like crostini.

"This is crazy," Bob said, more in awe than literally. "Charlie, how did you do this? This whole thing looks like an actual superhero cave. I thought you just did movies?"

Charlie shrugged his shoulders.

"I've done a lot in life, and wanting redemption is a powerful driver." He suddenly looked crestfallen.

Bob went up and hugged Charlie. "You look like you needed a hug." Charlie reciprocated.

"Hey, guys," someone said, stretching out the words in a friendly way. Bob yelped, slipped out of the hug, and looked toward the voice. A purple jump-suited man stood in the doorframe of the vault. The person, who was a bit taller and wider than Bob, slipped off his mask and laughed.

"What the heck, Bob? You don't recognize my voice?"

"Ned? Oh, I'm so sorry! Charlie was talking about villains and then you just show up and I wasn't ready. Like how many, you know, times, do you like, go to a secret cave with—"

"It's okay, Bob. I'm just teasing you."

Ned's fair skin was flush like he had gone running. His curly hair looked sweaty, and flecks of dirt and grime blended in with his freckles. His purple jump suit had similar wear with dirt and some flaky dried red substance. There were clear plastic tubes, one red and one white, running down each arm that connected to gauntlets made of wine corks.

"Bob," Charlie said, "meet King Grigio."

Ned took a bow. "Nice to meet you, citizen," Ned said. His voice dropped several octaves and boomed. Then Ned giggled.

"This is..." Bob said. "So cool!" His eyes ran back and forth between Charlie's outfit and Ned's ensemble. "Wait! Is that what my present is? What's my name?"

Ned cleared his throat then said, "We didn't—"

"What Ned is trying to say," Charlie interrupted, "is that we knew you ate chicken parm a lot. So, I used that as a starting point."

Bob spotted an angry glance Ned aimed at Charlie. It looked like Bob was going to have to play intermediary between them again. Some things never changed. Nevertheless, he wouldn't let it ruin this.

"Oh, I'm so excited!" Bob said. "Thanks, Charlie. This is awesome. And-and Ned! Sorry, I don't know if this was a Charlie thing, or you also designed it, but thank you, too." He ran up to the rest of his costume.

"We'll meet you by the computer," Charlie said with a wave and walked out of the room. Ned followed.

Bob stared at the costume. The suit called to him. It wasn't just because it satisfied his love of all things nerd and superhero, but also because he was sort of lost in life. Becoming a manager didn't thrill Bob. It was a direction, though. A goal of something other than the abstract concept of success and happiness. He couldn't see himself being happy at that job. It would only be part of his life, and hopefully Lila would occupy the other parts, so overall he'd be happy. Bob squeezed his fist. Maybe he wanted too much. A lot of people weren't happy with their jobs and still had happy lives. Was he being childish? No, but once again, Emrys was right. He was holding out for something and maybe this was it.

Buzz. His phone vibrated. It was a text from Lila. She wrote, *Sorry. Filming was crazy. See you this weekend!* Bob smiled. He had to do this. Lila was out there living her dream, and Bob was so proud of her. He had to live the same way.

Bob put the rest of the suit on. The mask was snug and smelled like a home cooked meal. Surprisingly, Bob's vision was unrestricted, and he could see clearly through the mask. Even breathing was easy. The pants were strange at first. The tightest pants he had ever worn were jeans, so having something press against every part of his legs took getting used to. On the wall behind his outfit mannequin was a sword with a crostini guard and a sub roll hilt. While the blade was metal, the guard and hilt were actual bread. The guard was so stale, it felt stronger than steel. The hilt, however, was as soft as freshly baked bread. Bob slung a leather back scabbard onto his back to hold his sword, grabbed two crostini throwing stars and some marinara grenades.

He felt ready. This was it. This was what he was waiting for. Bob wasn't destined to become a manager. Bob was destined to become a superhero. After one last deep breath to cool his overly excited nerves, he walked out to join his friends.

"Looking good," Charlie said as Bob approached. Ned turned around, more surprised that Bob had gotten so close.

"Dude! I really like the ninja approach," he said. "It feels like we each are going for a different like fantasy archetype. I'm the barbarian, Charlie's the knight, and you're the ninja."

"I didn't even think about it. These weapons just called to me. But also, are we allowed to have these? Like these are weapons. We can't just walk around the city like this, right?" Bob gestured to the weaponized marinara sauce in the form of a grenade. He had seen one in action back when he was an actor and knew exactly how dangerous it was. It had enough force to knock everyone to the ground and hot enough to give those people third degree burns.

Charlie turned back to the computer screen. "They're blunted swords. It won't cut anyone, but it'll sure damn hurt. Same thing with the throwing stars, and the guns just shoot liquid or pellets. So, if cops try to stop us, we aren't doing anything illegal."

Bob nodded in agreement even though Charlie obviously avoided his marinara grenade concerns. Since Charlie wasn't the kind of person who answered things twice, Bob let it go. He chalked it up to Charlie dancing along the legality line. Bob understood the life though. Back in the day, he downloaded songs without paying for them. He just hoped they didn't see cops. Bob's parents would kill him if he got arrested for running around being a superhero. They were horrified of anything ruining their yacht club reputation, and Bob being arrested wouldn't help.

"So, what do we do?" Bob said.

"I just got back, so I'm gonna sit the next run out," Ned said. "You'll stay here and get used to your gear. Train and stuff. Get the feel of everything and I can get you up to speed on what we've done and what we need to do. Charlie is going to patrol the streets. They're trying to get *Yumma-Gool* everywhere, and we can't let that happen."

"You know, I've been thinking," Charlie turned around to face them. "It's kind of dumb to keep Bob here, right? Like what better way to test something than in the field, you know? Where the action is."

Ned had an incredibly irritated look on his face. Bob gulped. Before he could diffuse things, Ned spoke.

"Charlie, you and I talked about this and agreed already."

"Aw, don't get your panties in a bunch. And Bob's an adult; let him decide." Turning from his brother to Bob, Charlie continued, "Bob, what do you want to do? Stay here or actually help people? People like Sergio. Stand up to villains."

Bob heard Emrys' voice in his head. Bob was afraid of confrontation but didn't want to be. Forget being a manager, he'd need to get used to it. He was in his mid-twenties and couldn't be a chicken all his life. What better place to start? He had Charlie with him. Bob tried to remember the people who drove those Raghu vans and what they looked like. No luck, but how tough could food distributors be?

"I'm in," Bob said confidently. He also smiled when he saw Charlie's approval.

"Great," Charlie said. "It's decided."

Ned said, "Bob, wait a—"

"Ned, he'll be fine. Bob's a big boy," Charlie said. "Go on, get your rest."

Ned clearly wanted to say something, but looked at Bob, then at Charlie, and finally took a deep breath. He slowly closed and opened his eyes, hiding any trace of his dissenting opinion.

Seeming satisfied with the conclusion, Charlie returned to the computer and pressed some buttons. There was beeping and bloops and the screen rearranged to show a live feed of docks. The screen had small, red, digital boxes that scanned people's faces, and the right side started listing out personal information, including a mug shot. "I can't see any of Raghu's boys here," he said. "It's just the usual drug dealers and fighting rings."

"Hang on. We're just going to let them be? They're criminals too," Bob said.

"Yeah. The cops can handle that. We focus on the crimes the police won't go after. Taste crimes, Bob." Charlie's head sank and his voice turned low like he was in mourning. "It started off with my favorite food cart. Abdel. He was my friend and the provider of my favorite Friday after work snack. He used to make it himself, but suddenly he was pushing this pre-made garbage. Then it was my deli. He'd make the matzah ball soup himself, then the broth was coming from a milk carton. One by one. Things were changing, Bob."

Ned's gaze slowly dropped. "Same things were happening to me." He looked forlornly at his friend. "You were so lucky for so long. We hoped it never caught you, but..."

"Reginald. He's behind all of this. He was some food distributor but turned to attack the things we love. I was walking back from work and saw his goons harassing some guy working out of a pizza window. I told the cops, but they didn't believe me. Then I got evidence, and you know what they told me?" Charlie punched the computer console. "They told me *there's nothing illegal about pre-made food.*"

Then it was silent. Bob stared at the two brothers with tears welling up behind his eyes.

"Enough of the sad stories," Charlie said. "Bob, you and me are going on a run. Ned, you stay here and radio us if you see movement at the dock. I'm gonna change, but I'll meet you by the couches. After that, prepare to fight crime."

Chapter Four

Bob and Charlie, each in their own uniforms, took off in his car toward the city. They didn't talk. Bob was in his own head, trying to figure out if there were any other places he noticed had changed. Sergio couldn't be the only one. Then he remembered the hot dog cart started using brand name buns instead of buying from the bakery across the street. There was also the diner he would go to late at night with his friends, who started using pre-made buns and not the ones they baked fresh in the back. It was like a switch suddenly flipped on in his head. All the impacted businesses were suddenly surging to the front of his mind. It wasn't just the food places, though. It was also the stores. All the local places he liked were emptier now. People opted for the big names or the chain stores, leaving the mom-and-pop shops to fend for themselves. He was no better than them.

"You okay?" Charlie said. He looked extremely out of place as he drove his modern car while wearing what looked like a full suit of armor.

"I guess. It's just scary, you know? Change. *Progress.* It's tiny things. Small little changes that hurt. Like, I might've stopped going to Sergio's because of something he didn't really choose. What about all the other places I abandoned?"

"I'm glad we caught you early. I turned my back on Abdel. When I eventually realized what was going on, it was too late. He had gone." There were a few silent moments before Charlie continued. "We are going to save Sergio and everyone else."

Once they crossed into the city, the car started driving at a normal speed and respected the flow of traffic. Charlie called it patrolling time. They didn't know who was going to be hit next. A lot of stopping crime was about guessing where it would happen or reacting to crime that had already happened.

People walked along the streets. Some looked determined, like they had specific destinations in mind and wouldn't stop for anything or anyone. Others looked like they had been partying all night. Even the tiny stores and shops they passed looked fine. Nobody lingered there too long or looked at a shop keeper menacingly.

"So, what happens if nothing goes down?" Bob said.

"Something always goes down. It's just about finding it. This city never sleeps, Bob. So that means crime doesn't either."

"Did you come up with that, or did you take it from some cheesy cop show?"

"Probably a bit of both."

After about 10 minutes of nothing happened, Bob turned to Charlie and said, "There's gotta be a smarter way to do this. Instead of just guessing. You sold popcorn and stuff, right?"

"When I was in the scouts? That was years ago."

"When you sold stuff, you went door to door. Maybe these people go door to door. Take out a neighborhood before moving on. Send the big guns after anyone who doesn't pay. Is there a pattern on the hit stores?"

Charlie stopped the car and parked on the side of the street. He pulled out his phone and called Ned.

"Hey," he said. "Bob is wondering if there's a pattern with the hit stores?" The idling engine muffled Ned's response too much for Bob to hear.

"Really...Okay...Yeah, send the address...Thanks, Ned." He hung up then turned to Bob. "It turns out they hit every store on the block except one. One is a holdout. Now, if I was a crime boss trying to take over a territory and one person didn't buy in," Charlie said, scrolling through the touch screen. He navigated to a map and a grid of the city popped up. They were only a few blocks from the spot Charlie was pointing at.

"You'd get them to comply...by force."

"We gotta move. Hopefully, we aren't too late." Charlie turned the car into superhero mode and blasted through the streets. Bob's stomach grew heavy, and a wave of nausea swept over him. He lowered the window, closed his eyes, and took deep breaths.

"Damn it. I'm sorry. Forgot about the whole motion sickness thing," Charlie said. "Just hang on for a bit longer."

The driving was much scarier with Bob's eyes closed. It was just a random series of honks and screams. Occasionally, there would be a violent crunch as the car tore through a street sign or slammed against a curb. Bob's heart was racing. Though the worst part was imagining his parents hearing about this. If Bob was arrested for vandalism *and* Reginald was involved, he wouldn't hear the end of that lecture. One time when Bob was a kid, he wrote April

Fool's Day in chalk on his neighbor's driveway. His parents found out, and he got an hour lecture on being a good boy. He never vandalized again.

It was going to be a long night.

After an eternity, Bob felt the car stop abruptly. He didn't open his eyes. His stomach kept sloshing, and the sweat was still going. Bob heard Charlie say something, but he interrupted with a raised hand.

"One second," Bob said. Slowly, his pulse slowed, and his stomach stilled. "Okay."

The two got out of the car and made their way into the rectangular store. The door opened with a bell ring. Bob could feel the clerk's eyes on them, even though they hadn't said or done anything. Their outfits were strange, so it made sense. Bob lived in the city for a while, and he never saw a knight and ninja walking around.

Bob headed to the right and sat at a table against the wall. There was a row of them reaching from the front to the back of the store. The deli counter occupied a large part of the store, forming an 'L' against the back and left wall. Glass displays showed off different meats, cheeses, tomatoes, and lettuce. Large chalk menus hung from the ceiling by the cash register. In the center of the store were a few shelves with snacks and simple meals.

Bob watched Charlie walk up around the aisles before joining him at the table. The cashier stared at Charlie, then the both of them once Charlie sat next to Bob.

"You were right. They weren't hit yet," Charlie said. He leaned in and whispered, "I saw a note on the calendar by the kitchen door. It said, *RR*. If Reginald shows up, you need to get out of here and get Ned."

"What? No!" Bob's tone sounded more like a hiss than a

whisper. He would not run away and leave Charlie to fight this battle alone.

"Bob, this is your first night. You don't have any experience, and Reginald is a bad dude. Plus, if *anything* happened to you, Lila and Ned would kill me." Charlie's face showed he wasn't exaggerating or leaving room for debate. Bob leaned back in his chair and crossed his arms.

He didn't like it, but Charlie made sense. Charlie was doing this longer and knew the equipment better. Bob would only get in the way if things got close. Fighting petty thugs was one thing. Reginald? His massive frame made him look like a truck. Bob pictured him standing behind the podium and making those jokes, but something was lurking below his booming laugh. Bob even remembered Sarah standing next to him. Her mouth opened in laughter, but her eyes never stopped scanning the crowd with a predatory detachment. They were dangerous people. Two sharks who smelled blood.

The door jingled again. Three men walked inside and headed straight for the counter. It was hard to see them past the shelves but they all looked like they were going to a rock concert. Bob looked back at the door and saw a woman walk in after. Bob's heart skipped a beat as she locked the door.

The woman had green spike hair with a black streak down the center. Her black leather jacket-covered body sloped out and down to stocky black jeans. The woman turned to Bob and Charlie and said, "You two might want to get out of here."

"Why is that?" Charlie said, turning to face her in his seat. "We were just about to order."

"Store's closed," she said, unlocking the door. "I'm not going to ask you again!" her voice thundered. The three others that had entered the store turned to the woman.

"Rachel, forget about those guys," one said. He had a wiry frame, liberty spike black hair, and an eye patch. "They won't snitch."

Rachel shrugged her shoulders, relocked the door, and approached the clerk. She pulled out a clipboard from inside her jacket and slammed it on the counter.

"Mr. Ross, my associates tell me you decided to...not buy our product."

"Y—Yes," Mr. Ross said. "I make my own sauce and don't want to force my customers to—"

Rachel slammed her fist on the counter, and it cracked. "Force. It's an interesting word," she said. "It's a very good way of convincing people, but it requires constant...reapplication." She gestured to one of her associates, who handed her a tire iron. She took it and shattered one of the glass displays. "See, people are scared at first, but people forget stuff. They tell themselves that the monster was in their head or *exaggerated*. That's why the monster, Mr. Ross, has to visit every once in a while. Can't let people forget. Now. Place an order so this monster can go back to her cave." She handed the tire iron back to her associate.

"Hey, butthead," Charlie said, standing up. "How about you leave that man be?"

Rachel's head snapped back, and she gave a surprised look.

"Easy there, Sir Dorks-a-lot. How about you and red boy sit down?" She turned back to the counter.

Bob nervously sprang to his feet, banging his thigh against the flimsy table.

"Ouch. Um—how about you—shut up, jerk." Bob scolded himself, even more so as Charlie slowly turned to him with a dumbfounded look.

"Oh, so the freaks speak! Peanut gallery must think

they're tough after graduating kindergarten. How about you shut up before I take away your recess."

Bob went to give a redeeming retort, but Charlie signaled for him to not even try. Instead, Charlie spoke.

"How about we take away your overpriced hair gel, you all-American reject?" Charlie then took an intimidating pose.

Bob was incredibly jealous of that line. Such a good superhero one-liner. In solidarity with Charlie, he slid his hand back and wrapped it around his sword. He didn't have much weapon training, just a bit from his actor prep. However, he had watched dozens of movies growing up. Some of it had to carry through. He gulped. Suddenly, Ned's recommendation to train sounded like a good idea. Unfortunately, it was too late to back out now.

Rachel turned back around.

"Mr. Ross, please hand me that. Yup. Thank you." She whipped around like a viper and hurled something at Bob. Right before it hit him, Charlie's hand teleported and grabbed it.

"Don't you know being salty is not in season?" he said, placing the saltshaker onto the table.

Rachel turned around and chuckled. Leaning against the counter, she said, "Lot of tough talk from someone who's been out of season for a thousand years. Get him!"

The associates sprinted forward, two to Charlie and one to Bob. Bob met his attacker halfway. The attacker jabbed twice. Bob double stepped backward, ducked, and punched him back, crushing his jaw. The attacker caught himself on the shelving, knocking whatever was left onto the floor. He steadied himself then thrust his leg forward like a javelin into Bob's chest. Bob stumbled backwards, shattering the cheap plastic table, the shards biting into his suit. The attacker stood, his shadow washing over Bob, and he snickered.

The attacker lifted a dazed Bob by the collar and continued the assault, with Bob being the punching bag. Bob felt the knuckles of the gasoline-smelling man hit every part of his torso. Bob struggled to push away, pressing his palm into the attacker's throat until he released Bob and gasped for air.

Bob grabbed part of the table and slammed it over the attacker's back, who fell to the floor and lay there motionless. Around the same time, Charlie finished his two enemies.

Rachel bit her lip and tossed off her jacket. "Looks like you're the one who's been messing up our territory. You wanna meet my boss or God? Your choice." She swung around the tire iron like she was warming up.

"I'm booked up tonight. I already promised a stuck-up biker I'd take her to jail," Charlie said. Another amazing superhero line! Charlie was such a professional.

Rachel took two steps forward and shoved the shelf into Charlie, knocking him back. She then hurled the tire iron at Bob. The shaft flew by his nose, so close he could smell the rust. It obliterated the store's window. When Bob turned back to face Rachel, he saw she held another shelf in the air. With a roar, she launched it at Bob.

He rolled forward to dodge it and got to his knee before hurling a crostini throwing star, the crust painfully scraping her cheek. She roared and stomped toward him. Rachel reached for Bob's throat. Bob tried to evade again but slipped on some spilt mayonnaise and failed to dodge.

Charlie burst into the scene and chopped her arm away. He followed with a hit to her stomach, then a rib. Before he could land another hit, she spun around him and cracked her fist on the back of Charlie's head. Charlie stumbled forward. Rachel stepped behind Charlie then slammed her heel into his back. He launched forward and collapsed on a glass display. Bob called out.

"Cha—Captain!" he said. Bob took a few steps backward and drew his sword. His hands trembled. This wasn't even Reginald. Bob hadn't even been a superhero for one night, and he was already losing. Charlie was out for now. Ned was miles away. Cops couldn't get here in time.

"Get her!" a child's voice said. Standing on the counter was a boy, no more than three years old. He had a towel around his neck like a cape and a sleep mask with the eyes cutaway.

"Get her, Chicky Parm man!"

Bob exhaled. His hands steadied, and he raised the tip of his sword. Rachel stampeded toward him. Bob danced out of the way, his feet gliding across the floor. She crashed into the door. Bob planted his foot on her back and pressed her harder into the frame. She pushed back, throwing him off balance. He regained his footing.

Rachel started hurling things from the nearby shelf at Bob.

"Get down!" he said. He used his sword to deflect all he could. It worked well until he cracked a can of soup against his blade, and broth shot out, blinding him. Then, Bob felt Rachel raise him into the air, turn him sideways, then throw him against the wall lined with tables.

Another plastic table shattered from his weight. He heard Rachel's stomps getting closer. She barked out. "Mr. Ross, sign the purchase order!" Bob pushed himself up slowly.

"Don't sign it," he said, then coughed. Bob drew his marinara grenade and, without pulling the pin, slid it across the floor. Rachel stomped on the grenade, breaking the glass shell, and slipping on the marinara inside. Bob caught his breath. His muscle ached, but they had been through worse. He forced himself to stand.

Rachel got up, too.

"You aren't too bad yourself. We'd love to have you in my crew."

"Your crew ruined my lunch. Your crew takes the love out of cooking to make a quick buck. Get out. Right now." His voice cracked.

Rachel shook her head and popped her knuckles. She ran at him with a cocked back fist. Bob swept her arm, and the blow went high. He punched her in the stomach then head-butted her. Rachel tripped and extended her arms out for balance. Bob launched two more punches, with one hitting each side of her face. Then he finished her with an uppercut. She fell backwards, where she didn't move.

"Chicky! Chicky! Parm! Parm!" the kid said, jumping on the counter. Mr. Ross's jaw dropped. The kid came down and ran to Charlie, who was groaning. "Are you okay, Mr. Spatchy Spatch?" He poked Charlie's helmet.

"It's Captain Utensil," Charlie said.

"Got it, Mr. Spatchy Spatch!"

"Captain. Utensil."

"Spatchy Spatch."

"Cap—fine, whatever." He flicked his wrist. "Mr. Ross, you should be alright now."

Mr. Ross's eyes almost exploded out of his head. "Alright? Alright? You got to be kidding me!" He swept a hand over the store. "You and that woman and that jerk. You all ruin my store! I could've just placed an order for 50 bucks and been done with it. Now I have thousands in property damage! How am I going to explain this?"

"You don't have to thank us," Charlie said. He knocked on the counter twice. "Chicky Chicky Parm Parm, let's get out of here." He walked out of the store. Charlie moved calmly, but Bob recognized the walk of a severely injured man and approached the counter once Charlie was outside.

Bob pulled a receipt from his wallet and wrote his number on the back.

"I'm really sorry about everything. This is the number for a pay phone by my house. Call if you need help rebuilding or those guys come after you again. Well...good night!"

He felt bad about lying since it was really his cell phone number, but Bob had a feeling a superhero shouldn't give out his personal phone number. This way, though, if anything happened or Mr. Ross was attacked again, they could hear about it right away. He carefully stepped over the knocked over soup cans, popped ketchup packets, and mustard bottles, fallen napkins, squished bread loaves, crushed chips, unconscious bodies, bug sprays, and dozens of other destroyed goods.

Chapter Five

"So," Charlie said as Bob got into the car. "First mission was tough, but you did great."

"Great? We got our asses kicked. We ruined that guy's store!"

"Yeah, but we kept Reginald's stuff off the streets. That's what matters at the end of it all."

"I guess." Bob glanced back into the store through the smashed window and saw Mr. Ross freaking out.

"Let's call it a night."

Charlie dropped off Bob at his apartment, along with his civilian clothes. Bob trudged up to the door, wreaking of food whose smells didn't go together. The people he passed looked like they were smelling a skunk. Even the people waiting for the elevator gestured for Bob to go ahead, saying, "We'll catch the next one. Oh yeah, don't mind. We are waiting for...someone."

Bob cleaned up and did a quick hand wash of his costume, leaving it out to dry over his shower. He collapsed into bed, turning quickly to his phone. Lila had sent him a picture of herself, standing in front of a calmed avalanche.

She wrote the caption, *another great scene.* Bob stared at the keyboard to write something back. She deserved something witty, but Bob's brain was fried. His muscles ached as he shifted in bed. Even his fingers were sore.

"Uh," he said then sighed. Bob wrote, *Next vacation spot?*

He deleted it.

You look powder-ful.

Deleted.

Bob sighed. *Perfect for a romantic ski-son.* Deleted. He let out a groan. *That looks like a fun vacation spot.* Sent. The phone showed she was typing something back, then it went away, dashing Bob's moment of joy at the idea of her texting back. He put his phone down and fell asleep.

* * *

Reginald ducked and turned sideways to fit through the front door of Mr. Ross's store. He wore his favorite blue and green floral Hawaiian shirt, khaki shorts, and brown leather sandals. Glass crunched underneath his steps. Sealed sodas exploded from his weight, their contents gushing over the store's floor.

"Quite a scene here, huh?" he said in a deep voice like the rumble of an earthquake. Reginald spoke every word with purpose and left a moment between each to let the authority sink in. Rachel, his subordinate, must've heard him because she began stirring. "Stay down. Please. Trash belongs on the floor. Same with the rest of you."

He continued his stroll through the convenience store wreckage until he reached the cash register. There was no one behind the counter, but he heard someone on the phone in the back. It was likely Mr. Ross. Reginald had difficulty hearing the conversation, but Mr. Ross sounded exasperated.

Reginald could relate to the feeling. Imagine his irritation after receiving the news that Ms. Rachel Lowby failed to persuade Mr. Ross to buy their products. To make matters worse, it was while he was enjoying a wonderful theater performance with his husband. There was no way he could make it back in time for the conclusion, but Reginald still wanted to resolve this quickly.

Reginald knocked on the counter. After a few seconds without a response, he knocked again. This time with more force.

"Excuse me," he said.

"We're closed!" Mr. Ross said from the back. The voice went back to the phone call.

Reginald growled. "Come out now, Mr. Ross."

The voice went silent. Reginald had that way with people. It was very rare he had to ask for something three times. The third ask was always so disrespectful and nothing made him angrier than disrespect. He raked his hand through his center part bowl cut and took a deep breath. The red vanished from his sight, and his breathing slowed. "Thank you," he said as Mr. Ross crossed into the store.

It was very common for people to tremble when they saw Reginald. Mr. Ross was no exception. Reginald towered over the already tall store owner, making him look no larger than a twig next to Reginald's tree trunk frame.

"H-h-how can I-I help you?" Mr. Ross said.

"First, our conversation would benefit from you getting control over yourself," Reginald said.

Mr. Ross nodded. There was no visible change in his demeanor, but Reginald continued.

"Excellent. Second..." Reginald looked around at the scene. "Was it worth it? Is my product so...abhorrent...that you trashed your store?"

"It wasn't me! It was—"

"Mr. Ross, I know who it was. I will ask for a second time. Was. It. Worth. It?"

Mr. Ross pursed his lips. He looked past Reginald, who traced his line of sight. The store was ruined. Tables were shattered. The shelves and goods were lying on the floor or thrown outside. Glass shards coated the floor. There were people lying on the floor, barely conscious. It would take weeks to recover and hours on the phone with insurance companies—truly a nightmare for anyone.

"Yes," Mr. Ross said.

Reginald spun around with wide eyes. "I think there must be a misunderstanding. Did you say *this* was worth it?"

Mr. Ross's confidence vanished as he nodded. The trembling grew exponentially as Reginald straightened his back and inched closer, growing ever more ominous.

"You're a brave man, Mr. Ross." He chuffed, his breath shaking Mr. Ross's hair. "I don't like brave men."

Crunch! Reginald's fist slammed through the cash register and cracked the underlying counter. For an instant, Mr. Ross looked at a crumbled-up receipt on the counter. Reginald slowly grabbed the receipt without looking away from Mr. Ross. He unraveled the receipt and noticed a phone number with a local area code written on the back. Reginald flipped it around and saw written on it was *Card Holder name: Bob Johnson.*

"Interesting," Reginald said. "Is this a customer of yours?" He stared at the receipt. The last name sounded familiar. He met dozens of people on a daily basis, but this name seemed very recent.

Mr. Ross nodded.

"A customer who leaves their phone number on a receipt for another store?"

Mr. Ross nodded.

"Do you take me for a fool?" Reginald's gaze crawled to meet Mr. Ross's eyes.

Mr. Ross didn't nod.

Reginald slipped the receipt into his shirt's front pocket. "Let us keep this information exchange between us Mr. Ross."

A woman walked in. She wore a heavy brown fur coat over a long sleeve red blouse and black dress pants. Her steps were light and careful as she avoided the floor's obstacles. Reginald looked at his reflection in her black sunglasses and smiled.

"Ms. Crafterson," he said. "Thank you for making time to join me."

She nodded. Ms. Crafterson then pulled out a purchase order form and rested it on the counter.

"Mr. Ross," she said. "We would like to inform you that our prices have gone up due to"—she looked at the slowly recovering goons on the floor—"increased labor costs." Her voice was as delicate as a babbling brook to Reginald. He had never seen her display anything other than control. She was the perfect business partner.

Reginald smiled, nodded, and turned to Mr. Ross, handing him a pen. "We look forward to a long and delicious relationship. Sarah, please have the crew bring in two cases of our finest squeeze bottle marinara."

Chapter Six

Bob woke up then reached for his phone. No text back from Lila. Was she mad at him? After texting her good morning, he pushed the thoughts aside and peeked at Charlie's text. *Round 2 tonight. Pick you up at* 3:00. Bob had off today, but he didn't tell Charlie. He groaned and went through his morning routine. However, this time, the manager training book sat untouched on the kitchen table. Instead, Bob used it to prop up his phone and he watched videos.

The speaker for the third video was a cop with a heavy Brooklyn accent. He said, "So, the best way to calm everyone down is to tell them they are *overreacting* and that you are going to tell them how they should compose themselves."

His partner gave him a nasty look. Bob agreed. It didn't seem like a good idea, especially since every other video he watched before that said the opposite. The internet wasn't very helpful most of the time. So, his video searching eventually turned to superhero movies and anime fight scenes. Occasionally, he'd checked his messages to see if he missed a notification from Lila. Nothing.

He got another text from Charlie. *Picking you up now,* he wrote. Bob texted him back. *What? I'm at work,* he wrote as he put his breakfast plate in his apartment sink.

I installed a tracker in your suit.

Bob stormed over to his shower and scoured every inch of the suit but couldn't find anything. After returning to his phone, he noticed Charlie had sent another text.

Jk, I put it in your phone.

Bob thought back to when he was changing into the uniform back at the hideout and left his phone on the counter. He wasn't sure if he regretted signing up for this yet. They did a lot of good, but Charlie was a pain. Bob now partly understood why he was on Lila's bad list.

Not even half an hour later, Bob heard the supercar's overly loud engine.

"Hey Bob! Get your ass down here!" Charlie yelled from the street.

He pouted his way down to the lobby and into the car. Then, the two of them sped away to the headquarters.

"Last night, I made you a new mask. Try it on," Charlie said. He reached into a cabinet in the lab vault and tossed Bob another brown mask. It looked exactly the same, except Bob could see there were rims around the eyes. Charlie continued after Bob slipped it onto his head. He said, "I installed anti-motion sickness glasses. They aren't super intimidating, so I hid them within the mask's fabric."

"I...feel the same?" Bob said. He was too tired to play along with whatever prank was going on.

"Well, that's good because it's for when you're moving. Like if we do another drive or fly somewhere—"

"Hang on, fly? Are we flying somewhere? I need to put

in PTO at least a month in advance, and I've been saving it up for going away with Lila."

"Ugh, you're so lame. What about the city, Bob? What about the people who need us?"

Bob bit his lip. He met their first fan last night. The kid cheering and smiling surged to the front of his mind. There were probably hundreds of kids out there that would look up to him. There were probably even more people whose businesses needed saving. It was selfish for him to just take time off.

"Get out of your head," Charlie said. "Come on, we need to train." They proceeded to a clearing outside and behind the boulder that formed the headquarters' entrance. It was a patchwork of grass, weeds, and dirt. While Charlie was pretty sure no one would see them, he wanted to be out of sight of anyone that stumbled onto the secret entrance. The boulder served as great cover. It was even larger than Bob appreciated the first night he came here, at least twenty feet high.

Once they were in the clearing, Charlie tossed Bob a wooden sword that looked exactly like the actual sword he had on his back last night. "I'm going to be honest. We barely survived last night." That was an understatement.

"So," Charlie said, "I figured you should practice with your new gear, so you can actually know what it does."

Bob frowned as Ned's warning popped into his head. It was Ned's idea that Bob should train and practice before going out into actual danger. Though, Charlie might not have done as well without Bob's help.

"Are you also practicing? Because you got knocked out," Bob said.

"Easy there, Bob. She got a lucky hit," Charlie said.

"If you say so," Bob said under his breath. It looked like

Charlie didn't hear it since he turned to a group of multi-colored mannequins arranged like bowling pins about fifty feet away.

He explained to Bob that they were for practicing with the marinara grenade. The blue ones were civilians, the green ones were cops, and the red ones were the bad people. Charlie shifted them around and presented various scenarios then explained the proper points for aiming to limit injuries. At first, the arrangements were simple. But after thirty minutes, mannequins dangled from clothes lines between trees with Charlie turning a wheel, so the villains were moving in a figure-eight pattern around the cops.

"Now it's time to protect them," Charlie said. He disappeared for a moment and returned with a wheelbarrow of different jars, cans, and bottles filled with condiments. He grabbed one, flicked it into the air and caught it like a baseball. "I'm gonna throw shit at the mannequins, and you have to protect them."

Seemed simple enough to Bob. They got closer to the mannequins, and Bob took a defensive position.

Charlie threw fast, but Bob was able to block most of the projectiles. It was a combination of deflecting them with the flat of the sword or swatting them away with the blunted edge. They completed a few rounds. Bob was getting the hang of it and excelling. He glanced backwards toward the mannequins to see his success. They were mostly still red from the marinara grenade practice with only small specks of mustard or relish.

As he turned back to Charlie, there was a flash across his vision. Bob flinched out of the way as the flash made its way toward the mannequin. Bob blinked and one of the mannequins didn't have a head anymore. Standing next to the decapitated mannequin was Charlie, holding his own wooden sword. "Round two. Protect them from me. By the way, heroes don't flinch."

Bob readied his sword, though this didn't go nearly as well as the other rounds. Charlie was vicious with melee weapons and Bob could only protect a couple of the mannequins.

After a quick lunch break, they moved onto the throwing star training. Bob stood on top of the boulder and saw ten wooden boxes, about five feet wide and tall, scattered around the dirt clearing on the entrance side of the boulder that hid the secret entrance.

"Sort of the same, sort of different, hit the bad guys, don't hit the good guys. Just put these on," Charlie said. He tossed Bob some wire mesh fingerless gloves and ankle warmers, which Bob hesitantly slipped on. Then, Charlie pulled out a remote controller, the kind you get with toy cars, and started pressing buttons in seemingly random sequences. There was a mechanical buzzing. One box's top flapped open and a single red balloon popped out.

"Really?" Bob said. He squinted and popped the balloon after a couple of throws.

Then the second wave of balloons came out, one of each color. One of his throwing stars scratched the civilian balloon, and it popped.

Bzzzzz! A jolt of electricity blitzed through his ankle. Bob yelped. "What was that!" he said.

"Negative reinforcement. Works wonders. Don't let the others slip."

This sucked. What happened if he hit the other colors? Was it worse if he hit a cop balloon? What if a bad balloon got away? Suddenly, Bob realized that one of the red balloons escaped, too high for him to hit. Both of his gloves zapped him. "I don't like this game!" Bob said with a pop of panic in his voice.

"They're getting away," Charlie said. He sounded like he was having fun, teasing Bob about his failures.

Bob popped the rest of that wave then started on the next one then the next one, and it ended two after that. There were plenty of failures along the way. His fingers looked swollen, but he couldn't feel them or his feet. Charlie said it would pass, eventually. Then Bob fell off the boulder and landed on his butt, which was perfect because it confirmed he could still feel pain in the other parts of his body. Charlie lifted him off the ground and carried him inside the headquarters.

"I guess I got a bit too carried away. Bright side though— your aim is way better," Charlie said.

"Being a hero s-sucks," he said. A lingering electrical current swept through his body as Charlie laid him on the couch. "I don't remember Doctor Time or the Masked Acrobat getting electrocuted."

"Well, they're pretend. Plus, they went through some trauma or had billions of dollars. *We* grew up in middle-class suburbs," Charlie said, taking a seat and slamming his feet on the table.

"What's wrong with that?"

"Nothing. We just don't have that gritty origin story that makes us exciting."

"I guess we'll just have to rely on our personalities and the things we do to get people excited."

Charlie huffed. "Yeah, easier said than done."

As his phone vibrated, Bob leaped to it. It could be Lila. He frowned upon seeing it was his landlord.

Dear Robert, there's a water leak. Sincerely, Harrison, he wrote.

Be right there. Thanks! Bob responded. Harrison was a little formal, but always kept an eye on Bob's place, which he appreciated. He also seemed to become extra generous when Bob paid him six months in advance.

"Hey, can you drive me back? I gotta check on my place," Bob said.

"Forget your apartment. We have to train! Reginald can attack at any moment."

"To be honest, I'm gonna be thinking about my apartment the entire time. I'll text you when I'm done, and we can jump between roof tops or whatever."

"Fine," Charlie said. Turning deeper into the headquarters, he shouted. "Ned! Bob's too good for training. We'll be right back."

Chapter Seven

"Mr. Ditkovich, you have an excellent tenant," Reginald said, turning off the phone and placing it on the kitchen table. Mr. Ditkovich said something back, but the kitchen rags Reginald's goons shoved in his mouth muffled it. He thrashed in the wooden chair, the legs thumping against the linoleum floor.

It was amazing what one could do with a name and credit card number written on a receipt. Robert Johnson was a loyal customer of Dos Pais's, the convenience store run by a Mr. Sergio Vasquez. After Mr. Vasquez joined Reginald's distribution network, they had access to his transactions, and from there, all he had to do was send a goon in and ask if Mr. Vasquez knew a Mr. Johnson. While Mr. Vasquez lied, his financial records could not. As an apology, Reginald suggested Mr. Vasquez purchase additional inventory, which Mr. Vasquez so graciously did.

Now Reginald stood in Mr. Ditkovich's first-floor apartment. It was cramped, but everything was cramped to Reginald. Even his penthouse felt small. Here, the kitchen, which was smaller than his bathroom, barely had enough room for the faux-wood round-top table and the accompanying four chairs though, Reginald appreciated the window overlooking a mini park. The living room had a couch along the back wall, a television a few feet away, and a hallway that led to the kitchen.

Normally, Reginald wouldn't attend to intimidation errands, but Mr. Johnson deserved special treatment. Furthermore, the stronger the message, the less likely he and his allies were to disrupt future Raghu operations.

They had time to waste while Mr. Johnson was making his way over there. His goons fully appreciated it. Some sifted through the fridge and the pantry, looking for snacks. Others were over in the living room, feet kicked up on the coffee table, watching a Ukrainian soap opera. While Reginald understood Ukrainian, his thugs did not know what the actors were saying. Instead of the plot, the attractive cast members kept the thugs entertained. It was one Reginald had not seen before, so it drew his eye more than the other goings on in the small apartment. There were bedrooms down the hall, but Mr. Ditkovich lived alone, and Reginald would not disrespect him further by invading his personal areas.

Reginald pulled over another seat from the kitchen table and translated for the others. They lost track of time as the story entranced everyone, except Mr. Ditkovich who continued to thrash about selfishly.

Knock. Knock. "Mr. Ditkovich? It's Bob. Are you there?" someone said from the other side. It must be Robert Johnson. Everyone went silent, and the television drowned out any noise from Mr. Ditkovich. There was another knock, followed by the sound of footsteps going down the hall. Reginald took out his own phone and dialed the number on the back of the receipt. Moments later, he heard a cell phone ring from outside the hall.

Mr. Johnson was a fool for providing his number. Regardless of whether it was incompetency or the extension of friendship, it would prove to be Mr. Johnson's downfall.

* * *

Bob walked into his apartment with two massive bags of paper towels. He stopped by the store, expecting the worst. When he realized his apartment was exactly how he left it, he was relieved and annoyed.

He tossed everything onto the counter, then texted Harrison.

Hey—my apartment's fine. What's going on?

Bob wished he had just told Charlie to hang tight. Now, he was going to get an earful about having to turn around when he was halfway back. *False alarm. Can you come get me?* he wrote to Charlie.

At least he got a break. He laid on his bed, turning all his attention to the ceiling. Then there was a knock at the door, heavier than what he was used to. Also, Harrison would have just texted him he was coming in and then unlocked the door; he never knocked. Was it Lila?

"Coming," Bob said. The Lila theory didn't make sense. She wasn't supposed to be back yet. Couldn't have been Charlie. He was way too eager to get back to training, despite his claims that he didn't need it. It couldn't be his friend Moni since she should still be teaching. He swung open the door and stumbled back.

"Mr. Johnson," Reginald said. His voice washed over the room like a principal calling out the troublemaker. He ducked to slip through the door frame, but his full height was terrifying. He was way taller up close, far more intimidating than how he was at his parents' yacht club induction ceremony, even in the red and white flamingo button-down shirt he currently wore. There was also a predatory gleam in his eye, which Bob didn't recognize before. "Had I known you were the son of Abigail and Greg Johnson, we could've had a much better meeting place. The club is wonderful in the early spring."

Bob kept taking steps back. Reginald's predatory eyes paired well with his haunting voice, a raspy, thunderous sound. The floors groaned under each one of his steps, so loud it drowned out the surrounding city. The world fell away, leaving the two of them, predator, and prey, alone in a void.

"Reginald," Bob said. "W-why are you here?" He already knew why. Reginald was here for business. As Reginald stepped closer, Bob stepped back. The dance continued until Bob tripped over the couch, falling over the armrest. He scrambled to his feet. Reginald simply walked past him and took a seat at the kitchen table.

"I'm here because I wanted to speak with you," Reginald said. He leaned back in the chair and feigned relaxation. All of Reginald's features focused on Bob, ready to pounce if he didn't behave properly. "You and your... associates...have been interfering with my business, and I'd like that to end." Reginald's gaze turned to the manager book on Bob's kitchen table. He flipped it open, unimpressed with the second he spent surveying the inside cover.

"It seems," he said, "like you understand business. Then this should be a rather simple and pedestrian discussion. I don't enjoy when people interrupt my business. Stop."

Bob had to remind himself to breathe. The superhero movies and books never talk about when evil comes to your door, how powerless you really can be when caught with your pants down. The Chicky Chicky Parm Parm suit was back at headquarters, and his closest ally was somewhere on the road between locations. Who knew if Charlie even looked at his phone yet and saw Bob responded to come back?

Reginald adjusted the chair, the floor screeching. Bob wondered how much time had passed while he was lost in his thoughts. Reginald's demeanor didn't change. He wasn't upset, nor did he look like he was impatiently waiting for an answer. He just sat there, like a lion waiting for the zebra to run, all too confident that it would catch the zebra.

Bob took a deep breath and said, "I'm...I'm gonna be honest. I don't like what you're doing to my neighborhood." Reginald's eyebrow raised, but he said nothing, so Bob continued. "For one thing, you're taking away people's choices in sauce. Sergio had been making his sauce from scratch for twenty years and you destroyed that tradition. You replaced it with really, really bad stuff. I tried it and it was the worst chicken parmesan sub I have ever eaten. Like...it was so bad."

Reginald growled. Bob's throat closed. He immediately regretted choosing to speak his mind. Bob was once again a helpless kid in middle school getting picked on by a bully. This was the part where the bully hit him or yelled back with something so much more hurtful. The same part where Bob would inevitably struggle to hold back his emotions.

Then Reginald's head snapped to Bob's phone, which had just buzzed. He clapped his colossal hands onto his thighs, sighed, then walked over to Bob's phone. "Bad, you say?" he said. Reginald crushed Bob's phone like a compactor, the pieces falling through his fingers like sand.

"The problem with people like you is that you're afraid of change. You cling to the notions of tradition instead of embracing the financial benefits of change, disruption. You ignore that Sergio no longer has to wake up an extra hour early to prepare the day's sauce. He no longer has to walk to the farmer's market and haggle for that day's produce. I made his life easier. You and he just fail to see that. You will though."

Right before he exited the apartment, Reginald stopped and said, "I know where you live. I know where your parents live. I know where your friends live. I know where your girlfriend lives. Hide? I will find you. Run? I will chase you. Anything but stop?" Reginald nodded his head and walked out the door, confident that his threat was communicated.

Bob sunk into the couch. He was powerless. All the bravery he had in the suit, fighting alongside Charlie, protecting his first fan, it was all gone. Could he do this? Reginald held Bob's entire life in the palm of his hand and showed his ability to crush it all. How much of it was a bluff? His parents were no doubt in danger. They went to Reginald's club several times a week. Reginald also had the contact information of Lila and all his friends when they signed in as guests at the yacht club. Bob was sick to his stomach. The room spun around him, and sweat poured from his face.

There was another knock at his door. "Excuse me?" someone said. Bob looked up, and there was a handful of people, wearing the same biker gang outfits as the ones from Mr. Ross's store. The one speaking was a guy, barely an adult, with a reverse Mohawk. "Bob? Yeah, Mr. Raghu said we had to rough you up," he punched the air playfully, "to let your associates know the message too. It'll be quick, but you looked like you were going through something, so we wanted to ask before we did it."

Bob stared in disbelief. He rubbed his temples and said, "Really? He didn't trust me to just tell them?"

"Oh, it's a 'them'? Is it like two people? Five people?" the man said.

"Get out!" Bob said.

"Eee—sorry. Can't let that happen. Like I said, real quick," he said then snapped a couple fingers. Three people crept into the studio apartment while the speaker stayed in the door frame, glancing back, presumably to see if anyone else was coming.

The three attackers, a woman with a buzz cut, another woman with dreadlocks and a man with a hair bun, slowly approached. Bob stood from the couch just as slowly. He had a home field advantage. He knew where the knives were, where his weights were, where the uneven floorboards were. The woman with the dreadlocks moved first.

Bob dashed to her, crouched, then swept the woman's legs out, toppling her to the floor. The man with the bun slashed with a revealed knife. Bob leaped backwards, the blade biting against the loose part of his shirt, and landed against the wall. The attacker swung again. Bob dipped to the side and tangled the man in the curtain string. Someone grabbed Bob and threw him against the kitchen table, knocking it over. Bob crab walked back, never taking his eyes off the woman with the buzz cut.

"Hold up. Bob, where'd you learn to fight like this?" the reverse mohawk man said. The attacks stopped.

"Acting classes," Bob said, catching his breath.

"Oh, right! You were that movie star! After we kick your ass, might ask for an autograph if that's not too cringy."

"No! Maybe? I'll think about it."

"I guess that's fair. Alright, well!" He snapped his fingers. "Guys, back to it."

The buzz cut woman approached cautiously with her guard raised. Bob got to his feet—

Crack. Something slammed into his ribs with splinters scattering to the floor. The reversed mohawk man appeared in Bob's peripherals. He shoved Bob up against the wall and continued the barrage. The rest of the gang watched and snickered. Bob tried to escape, but the onlookers shoved him back, and the speaker continued with punches and kicks. The numbness from his shock training helped ease the pain, but he still felt every blow.

"Bob!"

Bob instantly recognized Charlie's voice. The onlookers jumped and charged Bob's ally though reverse mohawk man stayed back. Charlie was dressed in his Captain Utensil suit and beat his arms against his chest. Then, he raised a staff with a strange tip. It looked like the tip of a trident, but the tips were all connected, making it look more like a...spatula.

The reverse mohawk man turned his attention for a second. Bob clapped his hands against the reverse mohawk man's ears and sprinted for the weights in the corner of the room. He grabbed the two lightest, hurling them at the speaker's thighs. They hit with a muffled thud against his legs, then an echoing thud as they dropped to the floor. Then the reverse mohawk man yelped and fell to the floor, clutching the bruise.

"Who throws weights! That really hurt! We were just doing our job," he said.

With a swift kick, Bob knocked him out and hogtied him with some exercise bands next to the weights.

Charlie looked like he was winning. His spatula staff swirled so fast it looked like a silver ghost was attacking the gang. They occasionally got in hits, but they would wince every time and curse Charlie's mighty armor.

"Boss!" the woman with dreadlocks said. She turned to face Bob with a snarl then attacked. "He was so nice to you!" Each of her swings looked like a haymaker, the whole mass of her body behind it. Sometimes she'd hit Bob, who guarded as well as he could. Other times, she missed and destroyed some fixture in his apartment. Seconds passed, and shattered lamps laid on the floor. The kitchen sink shot water out of the destroyed faucet and there was a hand shaped hole in his TV.

Bob couldn't find a chance to counter. They were starting another lap around the couch. The only thing in the apartment that wasn't ruined was the rug. The rug! As Bob retreated over it, he dragged his heel, making the corner flop onto itself. It was just tall enough to make the dreadlock woman trip, landing on the couch.

She yelled, but before she could get up, Bob knocked her out with a punch to the back of the head. Charlie finished his attackers around the same time, leaving each with a spatula welt mark on their faces.

"Thanks for turning around," Bob said, collapsing onto the couch. He let out a sigh then made peace with the fact that there was an unconscious person on his couch. He looked at her distantly, numb to the oddness of it like a bad art performance. Bob leaned back and closed his eyes. How did these people know when he was going to be here? The only people that knew were Charlie and....

"Harrison!"

"I'll go check on him. What unit?"

"103."

Charlie disappeared into the hallway, his armor clinking.

Bob chuckled as his muscles shut down. He put them through the ringer. Everything was trashed. Actually, the small cabinet under his TV was okay and so was his bed. At least he could sleep tonight. Bob reached for his phone to text Lila but frowned when he remembered he didn't have a phone anymore, and he didn't memorize Lila's number. Maybe Charlie had it since they acted together back in the day.

"He's okay," Charlie said when he walked back in. "They had him tied up, but he's fine other than some chafing around his wrists."

"Oh, thank God," Bob said. He didn't want people to get caught up in his mess. All this to protect some food.

Charlie shoved the unconscious woman off the couch and took her spot. "Are you okay?"

Bob struggled to sit up then stared at his friend as he digested his response. There were a million things going through his mind, and it wasn't like they were playing vigilante anymore. Things were serious. Reginald was a powerhouse, and a nasty one at that. His threats were sharp enough to take down his enemies, then he had his goons to clean up whatever was left. He was just a person, but it felt like he was pulled out of a comic book.

"I'm...I'm scared. He threatened my parents, Lila, my friends," Bob said. "If he...If he hurts them, I don't know what I'd do."

Charlie sighed. "He's slipped, and we caught him. He moved from food crimes to actual crimes, so the cops could take over."

Bob was still conscious enough to hear the reluctance, but honesty, in Charlie's voice. There was a 'but' coming, though Charlie stifled it. However, Bob knew what it was.

Bob said, "We don't know if these guys would rat him

out. Even if he gets caught, he still has that Sarah lady, right?" Charlie nodded.

"Yeah. She's just as vicious as he is. If we don't take down the whole operation, nothing is changing. Your family will be in danger, and all the small businesses will be forced to serve just awful food."

Bob couldn't live in a world where his kids and his grandkids never could experience a legitimate homemade sauce or a family recipe. Even if that wasn't at stake, how long was Bob going to run from the McCarthys or the Raghus of the world? Especially when they threaten his family. He had to draw a line somewhere. He had to stop running some time. Even if he was afraid, he had to fight back eventually.

Maybe it was residual electrical shock or maybe it was confidence, but something surged through Bob. His body felt like it was rebooting to life. Feeling returned to his feet then his hands. His muscles and joints were working again, despite the ache and bruising.

He turned to Charlie and said, "We need to take them down."

Charlie leaped to his feet, fist raised triumphantly in the air. "There it is! You take tonight off. Ned and I will patrol." He looked around the apartment. "Maybe stay at the HQ. This place definitely isn't safe anymore."

That wouldn't work. His friends and family would be in danger the moment Reginald found out about this. "I can't hide away while my family and friends are in danger. Lila is still out of town, but I have to warn her."

"I'll make a couple of calls to Lila's boss. I still have his contact info. He can call her and then get your family on a trip to something," Charlie said. "Come on, pack some stuff and let's get out of here. I got a feeling Harrison called the cops and I don't want to answer their questions."

A knot formed in Bob's stomach. "I can't run from the cops. I'll take a cab to you or something."

"A cab...To my *secret* base," Charlie said. After a quick contest of wills through stares, Charlie groaned. "Fine. I'll be in the car."

A few minutes later, there was a knock at the door, and Bob's hairs stood at attention. Bob was getting sick of people knocking on his door. There were a couple of cops, both of whom looked very confused and uncomfortable. Both were men, one old and leathery, and the other looked like a Wall Street bro that had a change of heart.

"Are you Bob Johnson?" the old one said after flipping through a notepad. Bob nodded.

"Oh, thank God," the Wall Street Bro said. "We tried like ten apartments before we got to yours. You have some very...strange neighbors."

"You couldn't tell which one was broken into?" Bob said.

"Well, we can now, but your landlord refused to tell us which was your apartment or even give us the damn floor," the Wall Street Bro said. Then he repeated in a crude impression of Harrison's accent, "He kept saying, '*I will not snitch!*' Then, we threatened prison, so he gave us a number. But it was a wrong one. That went back and forth a few times, so we figured we'd just guess." The old man whacked him over the head.

"Don't do accents, especially when they're bad," he said.

"But what about my *Australian?*" the Wall Street Bro said, dodging out of the way of another whack. "Okay, whatever. Fine. I'm Officer Mike Yates and this is my partner, Kevin Holt. We have a few questions for you."

Bob told his story, omitting Charlie's involvement. They didn't ask if anyone else came to the apartment, so it wasn't technically a lie. Nevertheless, his stomach turned to lead as he mentally debated whether this was wrong. Making matters worse, it was clear they weren't loving Bob's explanation. Sweat beaded around his forehead, and he became clammy. The officers looked all the more skeptical at him.

"So..." the old one said, "you're telling me you knocked out four people. By yourself. Then gave two of them a spanking with a giant spatula, which someone took, so you can't show us."

Bob nodded. That was definitely a lie. A tiny lie. It didn't hurt anyone. Bob felt the sweat percolate along his hair line. That was where it often started. Then the thought dawned on him that if he started sweating, they might realize he was lying. That made him start sweating in his arm pits. It wasn't visible yet. Bob just had to hold out. He just had to play it cool. They'd walk away eventually...Why hadn't they walked away yet!

"You know what? After all I've seen today, I think that's good enough," Kevin said. He flipped shut his notebook. "You're good to go. Mike here is going to look for evidence. You got a place to stay that's hopefully not here?"

"Yeah, I got a friend to let me crash at his...place," Bob said.

Mike rubbed his temples. "Just get out before we have to arrest you for lying. Don't leave town. We'll call you if we have a question." Bob had crossed through the door when he heard Mike continuing. "Is it just me, or are people getting dumber? How do you fumble that softball of a question?"

"Oh, Mike, me boy. That's a story as old as time," the old man said.

As the elevator doors closed, Bob heard Kevin exclaim, "You didn't get the guy's number. Damn it, Mike!"

Back outside, Charlie sat on the hood of his car when Bob walked out of the building. He said, "You are all good there? Conscious clear? Boy Scout mentality intact?"

"Weren't you the Boy Scout?" Bob said.

"Yeah, so why am I the one waiting for you?"

"We couldn't just leave," Bob said, his volume dipping toward the end of the sentence after realizing he didn't have the strongest point. It felt wrong. That's really all he could explain it as.

Chapter Eight

Abigail and Greg Johnson, Bob's parents, sat on the back deck of the Still Rivers yacht club, sipping on two cocktails. They clinked them together, made kissy faces at each other, then looked back out onto the water that stretched for miles with a long streak of brilliant orange in the center. Despite the chilliness, which they combated with coats and sitting next to the space heaters, they didn't want to be anywhere but outside.

Greg's phone vibrated.

Abigail said, "Oh, is it work again? These people are relentless!"

Greg looked at the caller ID then raised an eyebrow. "I don't think it's work," he answered. "Hello? Yes, this is him. Oh, hi, Reginald! Great to hear from you. Yes, we love the club." Abigail leaned in closer.

"That is wonderful to hear, Mr. Johnson," Reginald said. Even through the phone, his voice was so commanding and welcoming at the same time. "Ms. Crafterson and I would like to invite you to attend a function at the club this evening. Would you be available?"

Greg looked over to Abigail with a "should-I-say-yes" look on his face. Every part of Abigail's body gestured yes at the same time. The club was all about who you knew. She looked over at their tiny yacht dock and smiled. If they got in Reginald's good graces, the club would upgrade them to one of the premier spots. That would show those damn Worchestermins. This could also be a splendid opportunity to gloat. She whispered to Greg, so low that Reginald couldn't hear from the other side of the phone.

"Will the Worchestermins be there?" she said. Greg nodded.

"Will anyone else we know be attending?" he said.

Reginald chuckled. "No. No. It will just be the four of us. We would like the scene to be private."

Abigail pumped her fists in the air and danced on the deck. Joy wanted to burst from her lungs, but she held it behind her closed lips until Greg got off the phone.

"Wonderful," Greg said. "We will see you there at seven. We look forward to speaking with you further." He closed the phone and jumped up, matching her energy. Abigail giggled and didn't care who saw. They were having a *private* get together with the owner of the entire yacht club. She and her husband were going to rocket through the social strata. Let people judge them for getting excited. Soon she'd be above them. She smiled at Greg.

"I thought you said joining the club was dumb?" Abigail said. "That you'd rather be at home watching your shows?"

"Fine, you were right," he said. He stopped dancing around, but she could still see the happiness jumping from every pore on his body. "It grew on me. The food! The drinks! The boat! I love it all, and we are going to get even more! Unlimited guests! The founders club! All of it, baby!

I want it all." He sprung forward, wrapping his arm around Abigail's lower back, and kissed her on the lips.

Abigail fanned herself with her hand. "So, Mr. Dole has come to play?"

"Yes, he has," Greg said.

"Let me call Bob and let him know that we need to rain check on dinner."

Bob looked out the car window as they exited the city. They passed dozens of tiny stores, advertising the best pizza or sandwiches in the city. He wondered how many of them were in Reginald's web. There must be so many places that he wouldn't be able to enjoy. Then, he passed one with a familiar name, one that he had plans to visit tonight.

"Charlie!" Bob said. Charlie swerved the car then quickly stabilized it.

"What? What's wrong?" he said, looking around.

"Can I call my parents? I forgot I had plans to get dinner with them tonight."

"Yes. But can we limit the yelling, huh? I almost crashed. Julia, call Mrs. Johnson."

The car gave a verbal confirmation, then a dial tone came through. Seconds later, Bob's mom answered.

"Charlie?" she said.

"Hi, Mrs. Johnson," Charlie said. It was like decades washed away, and Charlie was the little kid Bob remembered. He sounded cheery and optimistic.

"It's so good to hear from you. This is unexpected," she said. Bob could hear his dad saying something irritable in the background. His mom then said something muffled in response.

"We'll have to catch up later, hun," she said back into

the phone. "Greg and I are trying to get a hold of Bob. We called him a bunch earlier, but our calls went to voicemail."

"Hey, Mom, sorry about that," Bob said. "I'm with Charlie. I can't make it to dinner tonight. Some stuff came up...with work."

"Did you get the promotion?" she said.

"No. Nothing like that. Just...have to work late. You know," Bob said.

"Well, that's fine. Something came up for us too, so this works out," she said. This time Bob could hear his dad murmur to *hang up the phone.* His mom hissed something back then softly giggled into the phone. "You won't believe it. We're having dinner with Reginald and Sarah! The ones from the club."

Bob forgot to breath for a moment. "No! Mom, Dad, stay away from them. They're bad people," he said. He could only imagine what his contorted and petrified face looked like. Reginald struck like a lion the moment Bob turned his back and caught Bob's parents in his claws.

"Bad people? Don't be silly. They're wonderful," his mom said. There was a third voice. Some chatting went on, but it was too low for Bob to hear. He turned up the speaker volume, but it was just inaudible mumbling. Then, after some rubbing against the speaker, which Bob recognized as the phone being passed, the third voice spoke.

"Hi, Bob? This is Sarah Crafterson. How are you?" she said. An eternity passed up between when Bob's heart stopped and restarted. It wasn't until Charlie nudged Bob that he realized he was supposed to respond.

"Hi, Sa-Sarah. I'm good," he said.

"'*Well*', Bob. You're doing 'well'. I just wanted to pass along a greeting from myself and Reginald. We look forward to meeting with you at some point. I only hope that you're as...pleasant company as dear Abigail and Greg, here."

Her words were like bee stings, a pleasant enough sound followed by pain. Charlie had pulled the car over and the two stared at each other. They weren't Charlie's parents, but the fear was apparent enough on his face. Bob would feel the same if the roles were reversed.

The only thing Bob wanted in the world was his phone. He had his parent's location and could just see where they were, or at least have a starting point. Bob could even have called Reginald or Sarah and just told them he surrendered. Instead, he was trapped in his mistake by the veiled threat of aristocratic monsters.

"You still there, Bob?" Sarah said. "I think we lost you."

"He's still here, Sarah," Charlie said. He countered her veiled threat tone with an arrogant one. "We'd love to join tonight. As the reasons the Johnsons are on your radar, I'd appreciate an extension of the same invitation. I do love a good red sauce."

Sarah went silent. Bob understood the secret message though he couldn't believe that Charlie was offering himself, his whole family, and all his friends to protect Bob's. Bob just shook his head, showing both his disapproval of the plan and subconsciously that he couldn't believe what was happening. Charlie just returned with a smile. *You'd do the same*, he mouthed.

"I will speak to Reginald, but I think that is a stellar idea, Charles," Sarah said. "We will send you the coordinates." *Click.*

The two collapsed back into their seats. Tension filled the car air, so thick Bob was afraid of saying anything. He lowered the window and took a deep breath of the evening breeze. Bob hoped it would calm him down, but there was still a hurricane in his head. He imagined so many scenarios, most ending badly and the ones that went well involved miracles happening.

Charlie looked no better off. He just stared straight ahead like he was absently watching a show rerun.

Then the car phone rang, startling both Bob and Charlie. Charlie sniffled, ran his hands over his face, and answered, sounding groggy. "Ned?"

"Yeah," he said, "you guys haven't moved in a bit, and we are getting lots of calls on *Yumagool* activity. Are you okay?"

"Ned, we have a serious problem," Charlie said, then sighed. "They got Bob's parents. I didn't protect his identity enough, and they identified him."

"God dammit, Charlie. I said this was a bad idea, and you didn't listen," Ned said, angrier than he had ever been before.

Bob said, "Guys—"

Charlie interrupted. "Quiet Bob. Ned, I know—"

"Charlie!" Bob said. "It wasn't you. I...I wanted to help that first guy, Mr. Ross, after we trashed his store, so I left him my number."

"Ned, we're gonna call you back," Charlie said, hanging up. He rubbed his forehead. "You're kidding, right? No trace. That's like rule number one of being a superhero. Because of that stupid move, everyone's in trouble."

"I know. I know I messed up. Bad. But—"

"But no. But no, Bob. We aren't in any shape to fight, but now we have to because we got made. There's only three of us. We needed guerilla warfare. A bunch of small fights in close quarters. We had the advantage." He punched the dashboard, withdrawing his fist with no sign of pain.

"Then I'll go alone. I'll tell them you were lying or something," Bob said. "You guys can just drop it all and your family will be okay." Before he could get out of the car, Charlie's hand whipped out, and he yanked Bob back into the seat.

"That's stupid, Bob. I'm angry, but I'm not leaving you to him," Charlie said after a moment of staring out into the city. "This had to come to a head eventually. More time would be nice, but it would mean more casualties. More lost recipes and traditions. He wasn't stopping at *YummaGool*. I saw evidence of other markets, even other gangs, doing this. They grew faster than we could, so this really is it."

Bob stared at him, but Charlie never stopped looking ahead. They weren't on a busy street, but it felt emptier than it should have. It was like the city itself was aching, a piece of it taken away.

"I've messed up a lot, Bob. You've seen part of it. Lila and Veritably won't forgive me for what I did, and that's fine. This was for me, though. So, I could forgive myself. Use what I learned from the studio and help the everyday people. Stop the crimes that the laws weren't designed to fight."

Bob could feel the tears well up behind his eyes, but he held off. Reginald's activities also sounded like extortion, which was already illegal, but Bob figured Charlie knew better and didn't mention it.

"We," Bob said, "You. You've done a lot, Charlie. You've been doing this for months, and I can't imagine how many stores you've saved, how many people you've inspired. However this goes down, you should appreciate it."

Charlie started up the car. After notifying Charlie's parents of what was going on, they drove back to the headquarters in silence, nervously waiting for Reginald's text to come through, the text that was going to mark the end of the story.

When they got back to headquarters, Ned was at the base of the computer staring at the screen. It displayed a map of the city. Red blinking dots covered it like pepperoni covering a pizza. Several of the dots had names and mugshots attached to them. He spun around, terrified.

"This is bad. This is so bad," Ned said, sounding out of breath. "I've never seen so many reports. Reginald's gang has mobilized and is hitting ten stores at once and moving fast."

Bob and Charlie jogged forward and gazed in awe at the screen. One of the moving dots was Rachel, the woman Bob met his first night. According to the computer, she was attacking a store a few blocks from Mr. Ross's. There was a dot over Mr. Ross's store, too. Bob hated knowing that Mr. Ross might've called his phone, and he wasn't able to answer—all because he was careless and got caught. There was a dot over Sergio's store, too. Then a few dots over small Chinese and falafel places that Bob knew.

"They're expanding their reach too. We got calls from Ren's Garden, Chickpea Sister, and Big Winers. They're pushing boxed wine, Charlie. I thought we had months before their boxed wine was ready to move."

"Move over," Charlie said. He gestured for Ned to move aside, took the seat, and typed furiously. "We haven't gotten a text from Reginald, so it's making me think he's still got Bob's parents in transit or he's waiting until he can get ours before meeting. In the meantime, we have to do our job. We have to save the city."

Ned took a deep breath and swallowed whatever he wanted to say. Bob frowned. They were usually good at conversing. He got the feeling they were going to explode on each other. Bob just hoped it wasn't at a bad time.

Bob made his way to the armory. As he switched into his hero costume, he surveyed all the bruises and cuts on his body, some small, some swollen, none of them pleasant looking. They didn't feel pleasant either, radiating a painful buzz as the costume's seams slid against them. However, when Bob slipped on the mask, all the things holding him back vanished. He was Chicky Chicky Parm Parm, defender of the red sauce and protector of cuisine. He wasn't the scaredy cat that couldn't cut it in retail.

Soon after, Charlie and Ned came in and adorned their own costumes. They operated silently and emotionlessly, their eyes never moving away from their outfit or gear. The only sound was the muffled beeping of the computer alarms and the ruffling of the gear as they equipped it.

Bob anxiously waited on the couch in the center of the hide out. The ominous computer beeps had only grown more frequent. He imagined the horde of thugs storming store after store, forcing them to buy whatever Reginald was pushing.

"Bob," Charlie said. "Let's go over the plan."

They regrouped by the computer. Charlie explained the plan. Each of them was going to operate on their own tonight. If they could take down whoever was in a particular store, then they should. If not, they should provoke Reginald's gang enough to give chase and buy the store owner some time to lock up. If the store was closed, they couldn't push their products.

The three of them also briefed Mr. and Mrs. Lorox, Ned's, and Charlie's parents, to stall Reginald and Sarah for as long as they could. Once Reginald or Sarah captured their parents, they would send a text to Ned about their location. Charlie also gave Bob a burner phone, so they could stay in contact.

"It's got both of our numbers," Ned said, gesturing to himself and Charlie. "Fully charged up, as are ours, so communicate when we can. It's linked up to the headpieces in our suits, so it should be easy."

"Charlie, Ned," Bob said. "Thank you." Both nodded back and smiled.

"Hands in the middle. Save taste on three," Charlie said. "One. Two. Three."

"Save Taste!" they said in unison.

Moni let out a yawn and went down her apartment stairs. The elevator broke again, so she had to take the stairs, which were cast in a dingy green light. The area smelled just as dingy, like someone trapped the rain smell in the stairwell, and it turned stale. This late, normally she'd just stay in her apartment and relax, but she ate a pot brownie and was out of snacks, so she had to run out and get some.

The makeshift doorman, a raggedly looking man that sold her sleeping medicine and was probably the same age as her, looked up and smiled so hard it made his eyes look closed. Moni wasn't too sure if the landlord actually hired him or if he just posted up in the lobby. Either way, he was nice, so Moni didn't complain.

"Hey, Moni," he said, his voice dragging every syllable. "Just like be careful out there, you know? Been seeing some weird stuff." Moni glanced through the glass panes lining the wooden door out to the street. She couldn't see much, but noticed there was a bit more hustle in the people going by. It wasn't fear, more like they saw something they didn't want to deal with. She turned back and gave him a thumbs up.

"Thanks, man," she said then exited.

Her favorite spot was a couple of blocks south of her apartment, run by an old guy, Mr. Kwok. He always nagged her, but in a caring way. It kind of reminded her of her dad, but Mr. Kwok was Chinese and way older. He didn't provide the best range of snacks, but he gave enough. She mostly liked his store because of him. Moni appreciated finding good people in the city since they were rare.

She jogged across the street, noticing there were a lot of biker-gang-looking people, not the friendly-retirees kind but the kind that look like they were going to beat you up if you crossed them. They wore the stereotypical leather jackets, silver studs on their shoulders, embroidered cloth patches on their chests and had wild haircuts. Moni took another look and wondered why there were so many prowling the streets. This was a hipster neighborhood, so it was rare to see any motorcycle bikers. She was even more curious why they were hustling between convenience stores and blue vans with the name *Raghu Distribution* written on the side. On the street, they were polite.

But then, they would enter stores with boxes of food, clear the shelves of whatever was on them, then stack whatever food they were carrying. One group carried milk crates of organized red tubes that reminded her of toothpaste tubes. Another group had a box labeled *Microwavable Rolls*. She shuddered. She had tried one before. They were chalky, mushy, and bland at the same time. Her old deli started pushing them, so she had to stop going.

Moni pulled out her phone and texted her friend, Bob. *Dude, weird night. These biker guys are like running the food delivery business tonight.* She then realized that she had sent Bob a bunch of texts, and he hadn't responded to anything in a few hours. She followed up her last text with *hope you're okay*. Then she slipped her phone into her pocket.

Mr. Kwok's store, Knight Grocer, had the same bikers inside. There were a handful of them, one at the counter, toward the back of the store. The one at the counter talked to a concerned-looking Mr. Kwok. The rest paced up and down the aisles. The store shelves were barely shorter than them, but short enough that she could only see the bikers' eyes and hair. She promised herself to be quick, so she darted to the freezers on the far-right wall.

The conversation between the biker and Mr. Kwok didn't sound pleasant, but the smooth jazz playing over the store's speakers stopped her from hearing more than snippets. She heard "shipment", "order", and "better". She was so enthralled that she didn't notice one biker was walking by her, and she jumped when he opened the freezer next to her.

He had spiked hair, dyed to look like an orange peel, which matched the orange contact lenses he wore. His jacket was sleeveless, and he had tattoos of various orange things like oranges, pumpkins, fall leaves, which contrasted well with his dark skin.

Moni gave him a nervous smile then spun around and darted to the counter, never making eye contact with anyone else. She waited in line behind the biker who spoke to Mr. Kwok. He had a similar color to them but chose purple. Moni also hadn't appreciated how tall he was. Mr. Kwok was her height, but the counter was on a platform about a foot higher than the ground, so Mr. Kwok usually looked down on his customers. Still the Purple Man was looking down on Mr. Kwok. There was a plastic barrier on the counter separating the two of them, but judging from the size of his arms, the Purple Man could probably smash through it.

"Thanks for doing business with us, Mr. Kwok," Purple Man said. "My buddies will start clearing out your shelves and freezers to make room for your shipment." He whistled. "Blue! Green! Three cases of *YummaGool* and two boxes of *RisingRolling.*"

Two men appeared from within the aisles, one covered in blue and the other covered in green, exited and returned with what Moni assumed were the orders. The Purple Man turned to see Moni, scanned her face, then stepped out of the way. He snickered at Moni and said, "You might want to put those back. Knight Grocer is about to get some premium snacks."

Moni regarded him for a moment, decided not to respond, then turned to Mr. Kwok.

"Hey Mr. Kwok, how you doing?" she said, mostly out of habit. It was very apparent from his downcast face and slow movement he wasn't doing well.

"Busy," he said through a forced smile. "You know how things are. Changing times. People want new things. No one is happy with..." His voice trailed off as Purple Man turned to look at him. "I'm just busy."

Moni took a small step away from the Purple Man, who hovered to her left. "Yeah, busy isn't fun. I appreciate you, though."

Bruuring. The door chime rang, and Moni turned around. She immediately pulled out her phone and snapped a picture of a chicken parmesan looking hero standing in the doorway. Moni thought she was hallucinating when she considered the facts. Biker thugs in rainbow colors surrounded her. Smooth jazz played on the speakers. Someone in an outrageous red and brown uniform stood in the doorway with a bread themed sword raised.

She sent the picture to her friend Bob then leaped over the counter next to Mr. Kwok. "Hope you don't mind, but I don't want to get in the middle of this."

Chapter Nine

Bob froze for a second as his friend, Moni, slid over the counter and to the other side behind the plexiglass barricade. He didn't expect to see her and wasn't sure if Reginald's thugs were here for the store, her, or both. To be safe, he didn't acknowledge her. Reginald knew his secret identity, but judging from how the thugs reacted, it didn't seem like they knew.

"Hey, Mr. Tights," the man by the counter said, his purple ensemble being the focus of Bob's attention. "Hey! I'm talking to you."

Bob hadn't heard of that group before. They must have recently joined Reginald. He opened his mouth to respond, but he didn't want Moni recognizing him. He gulped, shifting his Adam's Apple to lower his voice. "Halt, criminals!" He sounded dumb saying it and criticized himself internally. "Stop what you're doing right away and leave. I will take your cooperation into..." Bob noticed the other thugs gliding through the aisles like sharks, their wildly colored hair looking like fins. He took a step back, bumped into the door and startled himself.

"Look at this guy," the Purple Man said with a chuckle. "Think he can take all of us. Let's show him otherwise, Rain-Bo's!" A chatter of chuckles came from the rest of the colored thugs, one orange, one blue and one green, as they got closer.

Bob drew his crostini sword and held it at his side with both hands, fingers gripping the bread hilt tightly, crust cracking as if to say it was ready to fight. "Bring it on," he said, still altering his voice.

Orange Bo hurled items from the shelves at Bob, which Bob sliced through with his sword, and the contents exploded out. The floor was suddenly slippery with soup broth and bean juice. Bob planted his feet and continued his defense. His training prepared him for things just like this. He could handle it. Nothing could stop him.

Suddenly, Blue Bo charged from the side, shoulders lowered, like a bull. Bob spun on his heel, stepped out of the path, then brought down the blunt blade edge on Blue Bo's back. Blue Bo lost his balance and crashed violently into a cardboard sponge display.

Orange Bo continued his can barrage. A can of tuna hit Bob on the back of his neck, then a jar of cheese sauce smashed his nose as he turned around. Bob winced and covered his face. He dashed up against the other side of the aisle for cover. It shimmied as his weight hit into it. Bob smiled.

He put his sword down, squeezed his body under the middle shelf, then wedged his arms underneath. Bob pushed up as hard as he could, like he was trying to power clean the shelving, and the top of the shelving leaned back. Bob strained to push harder, his thighs trembling. With an ominous metallic groan, the shelving tipped over and fell onto Orange Bo, who couldn't escape in time. Orange Bo yelped then fell silent.

The shelving tipped over into the next aisle, knocking the next aisle's shelving over then the next aisle's shelving until it all fell onto the far wall. Bob could see the counter, where Moni stood filming everything. He gave the camera a thumbs up and—

Whoomp!

Something hit Bob like a truck and slammed him into a wall of unopened cardboard boxes. They were sturdy, and the corners stabbed into Bob, which hurt more than being tackled. The something was Purple Bo, who shoved Bob again, so Bob faced him. Purple Bo snapped his forearm to Bob's neck and pressed. "Night, night, you red idiot," he said.

At first, Bob focused on the pain that seemed to collapse his throat. Then, when he went to breathe, Bob panicked. Nothing was getting through. It was like Bob forgot how to use his lungs. He gasped and gasped, but he was forgetting something. Bob reached for anything he could. His eyes raced around the room for something to save himself. His heart slammed against his ribs like it was trying to break out and save itself. His ears buzzed, then felt muted, like he was going into an underwater tunnel. Then Bob's eyelids fell heavily. They dipped, but he forced them open. They dipped again. Bob kept them open, but it was a little harder.

Thwack! Life surged into Bob's body, and he came to, kneeling on the store's scratched up white linoleum floors. The air felt like fire when he inhaled it. The pain went all the way to his stomach. It took almost all his strength just to lift his head and for him to realize he was staring at the back of Purple Bo's knees.

Purple Bo, who faced away, said, "You on his side? You

think you're tough?" He sounded like a blood thirsty werewolf. A woman responded with a competitive energy like she was smack talking at a sports game.

"You think you're tough? I'm a damn elementary school English substitute teacher. You think *anything scares me?*" the woman said. Her voice was a dead giveaway.

Moni?

Bob struggled to his feet and saw his friend standing on the other side of Purple Bo. Green Bo and Blue Bo also surrounded her. Moni didn't flinch, the spitting image of a superhero herself. She stared into Purple Bo's eyes like it was a contest.

"I like you," Purple Bo said, breaking the silence. "You walk away now, and my boys here won't totally beat you up."

Moni, her face only showing animosity, said nothing.

Bob took a deep breath, then cleared his throat. Nobody reacted. He cleared his throat again, louder. Still, no one reacted. Everyone must be too distracted by Moni's lioness aura and the jazz music playing over the store's speakers. Bob rolled his eyes and tapped on Purple Bo's shoulders.

Purple Bo whipped around and looked surprised. Bob waved then punched Purple Bo across the jaw, which sent him flying into the shelving wreckage. Moni slipped out between the other Bo's, who didn't seem to care too much as they ran over to Purple Bo.

Purple Bo groaned as he rubbed his chin. After he realized what had happened, he swatted away their help and yelled. "Get them!" he said. Blue Bo chased after Moni, who ran away. Green Bo jabbed at Bob, who blocked the blows with his forearms. Bob stayed on the defensive, only taking a few hits, and dodged until he maneuvered Green

Bo to the large puddle of canned soup and bean juice by the front of the store.

Bob grappled Green Bo then tucked his leg behind Green Bo's. He pulled out his opponent's leg, and the two toppled, with Bob landing on top of Green Bo in a messy, squish sound. The two struggled, but Bob landed a finishing blow and knocked him out. Bob leaned back and saw Purple Bo was trying to rescue Orange Bo from the shelving.

Bob leaped to his feet, hurling a marinara grenade at Purple Bo. The grenade exploded as it landed on Purple Bo's chest and knocked him backwards. Purple Bo yelled out in pain as the marinara sauce burned any exposed parts of his skin, including his face, which seemed to hurt the most.

"Hey, you!" someone said.

Bob turned to see Blue Bo holding Moni with his arm around her neck. She looked miniature compared to him. Moni thrashed, but once Blue Bo squeezed harder, she focused all her attention on pushing back against his choke hold.

"Drop all your stuff and help my friends up," Blue Bo said. "Or I'll snap this lady's neck."

Moni said something, but her voice was too stifled to be audible. Instead, it sounded like she was gargling.

Suddenly, Bob noticed the store owner waving and pointing at a fire extinguisher. Bob had to stall.

"Hey...um...you know Blue's my favorite color."

"Really?" Blue Bo slightly relaxed.

"Yeah, like totally. Super cool color."

"Right! It's literally a 'cool' color, like a cool paint color. I just want to give off that vibe of peace and stuff."

"Oh, yeah, I'm totally getting the vibe that you're peaceful."

"If you want, I can hook you up with my guy. We can get that outfit color swapped." At this point, Blue Bo's guard was totally down. If he wasn't so strong, Moni could've slipped out.

"Eh, never seen a blue chicken parm sandwich before."

"Between you and me, Raghu Distribution's got that coming out in a few months."

"Hit the bastard!"

Suddenly, the store owner stood behind Blue Bo with the fire extinguisher. He bashed Blue Bo over the head with it, and the thug collapsed like a house of cards. Moni wriggled herself out from the grip of the unconscious Blue Bo and lay down on the floor.

"I...love...this...city," she said. Moni sat up and pulled out her phone. She was texting away then looked up at Bob. "Mr. Superhero guy. What's your whole deal?"

"Bad people are making stores carry bad products," Bob said. "I'm here, so they don't do that."

"That's super cool. Let me stream you." Moni raised her phone then gestured for Bob to talk.

"Like right now?"

"Yeah."

"What should I say?"

"I don't know. You're the superhero, right? Aren't big speeches like what you do?"

"They do in movies, but they have writers telling them what to say."

"Okay. So just copy what they do."

"I'm not a good public speaker though. I don't do well with attention."

"It's just you, me, and Mr. Kwok. No one else around."

"Okay, you're right." Bob quickly exhaled. "I got this."

"Come on, Chicken Parm guy."

Bob cleared his throat.

"Dear people of this city, there is a menace in our streets, a villain devoid of taste, and his only goal is to destroy what makes our city what it is. Bodegas, delis, and stores all across the city strive to bring their own spins, create their own flavors. This villain is trying to take all that away. This *villain* wants me to eat garbage." He raised a toothpaste-shaped tube of *YummaGool* to the camera. "I don't want to live in a world where my kids only know red sauce out of a toothpaste tube. I want them to know that their favorite store makes the sauce fresh with love and ingredients from local places. I want them to know that every sandwich, every entrée, every dip is made unique. If you want that same future, stand up. Stand up to these, these thugs who are trying to take it away. Go down to your corner store and help us fight back!"

Moni bit her lip and crunched her face. It was the face someone makes when they really messed up and don't know how to say it. Bob's eyes went wide.

"What happened?"

"I...I forgot to record it."

"Oh, well, that kinda sucks. I thought it was a good speech. Well...I appreciate the effort," Bob said.

Then Moni's face turned mischievous, and she said, "Just kidding!" She tapped on the screen and started recording herself. "You heard the man! Get out and fight, people!" Moni put her phone away then leaned back against the refrigerated wall, which was covered in exploded food liquids. Bob winced at the thought of what the concoction tasted like.

The store owner reached behind the counter and pulled out a newspaper. He showed the front cover to Bob and said, "Are you him? Are you Chicky Chicky Parm Parm?"

The newspaper was the *Deli-cious Times*, and the cover page article was talking about three superheroes who have been protecting local stores. There was a quote from a young boy, Arnold Ross, age 4. *He was so cool! He, like, punched the bad lady and saved my dad's store. I wanna be him for Halloween. Spatchy Spatch was cool too, but he was taller, so my brother can be that one.*

Bob smiled. He was thrilled to have the mask because it soaked up his tears. The last couple of days had been brutal, and every part of his body hurt and being choked out didn't help. To know he was making a difference like that, mobilizing an entire community, made it all worth it.

Moni's unrestrained laughter ruined the moment. She laughed so hard she was gasping then laughing quietly because she used up all the air in her body. Between breaths, she said, "Chicky. Chicky. Parm. Parm!" The store owner playfully kicked her.

"Cut it out! This man saved my business. He and his friends are saving the city!" he said. "You, Chicky Chicky Parm Parm, eat for free. Whatever you want, come by and it's yours. Well...maybe a few free things. I still gotta pay to fix all the damage you caused."

Bob gave a thumbs up and said, "That seems fair." He then realized he didn't disguise his voice.

Moni stopped laughing and sat up with a confused look on her face. "Are you..." Then her eyes went wide with recognition, and she excitedly slapped the floor a bunch of times. "You! You're—a hero." She gave a playful wink, then wiped away a tear. "Okay, Mr. Kwok, let's get started on cleaning up. Chicky Parm—whatever the hell his name is— has a city to save."

Chapter Ten

Bob returned to the fight out in the streets. He liberated one store after another. Store owners and thugs alike called out his superhero name when he entered the store. Bob was a red gust of justice as he took out criminals and defended the stores.

After protecting his fifth store, he got a phone call from Ned.

"Hey! What's going on?" Bob said.

"They got my parents. Reginald said to meet him at the Sunside Piers." He sounded emotionless, like he was poorly holding back a dam of tears.

Sunside Piers were a busy and massive hub of bars, businesses, and warehouses. It would be busy at this time of night with people visiting the bars and cops watching for late night illegal shipments. That meant Reginald planned to take them to a secondary location, which was never good news. Cops and investigators rarely found people who moved to a secondary location. Bob didn't have a choice, though. The mess he caused now involved both his parents and Ned's parents.

"I'm so sorry, Ned. It's my fault they're in this situation."

"We can blame later. Where are you?"

"I'm on Jesper street and Knot. I'll tell Charlie to pick me up."

He heard Charlie's car before he saw it. The engine's sound ricocheted off the walls and struck fear in the thugs' hearts. All the ones he saw ran in opposite directions, which he was happy to see since he wanted to conserve his energy. The constant fights, running around, and lack of sleep took their toll.

The car came to a screeching halt. Ned lowered the passenger side window, letting out an unholy stench of dozens of different foods, sweat and blood, some of which were his own. Charlie was in slightly better shape, probably from his metal helmet. There were nicks and scratches on his face, his knuckles red. Ned had a black eye, welts, and long cuts along his arms. Some sticky yellow substance matted his hair and stained his hairline. They both looked tired.

Bob enjoyed the last moments of fresh air and hopped into the car. They sped off to Sunside Piers.

After arriving, they puttered into the fenced off area, beyond which he could see almost a hundred of Reginald's men walking around, muttering to each other. There were two operating the gate. After peeking into the car, they waved Charlie in, and he drove through slowly.

The thugs sneered and whispered among themselves. Once they spotted the car, they seemed to wait until the last moment to step aside. There were so many of them, and they were so densely packed. They snickered and hollered at the superheroes. Some even banged on the glass and kicked the sides of the car.

Then they saw Reginald. He sat on a crate in a new Hawaiian shirt, purple with pink salmon covering it like polka dots, but everything else about him was the same. Same bowl haircut. Same khaki shorts. Next to him was Sarah, who also sat on a crate, dressed as elegantly as the last time Bob saw her at his parent's yacht club induction ceremony. Her hair was drawn backward and flowed out over the front of her shoulders in dark curls, layering on top of her gold sequins dress that looked like a disco ball under the car's headlights.

Bob, Charlie, and Ned got out of the car. Reginald turned to them, with a disappointed principal look on his face. Sarah also turned to them but looked offended by their presence.

"Good evening," Reginald said. "Gentlemen, you appear to have been busy. Robert, you can't imagine my surprise to learn of your involvement in tonight's vigilance, despite my orders for you to refrain." He chuckled to himself. "How foolish to expect a fool not to fool? I initially thought your...confusion...was from my lack of specific instructions, but I combed over my words, reimagined every moment in my mind and came to the conclusion that I was *very* clear. So maybe I failed to give you the proper motivation, but again, you seemed sufficiently scared when I threatened your parents, your friends, and that woman. Lila? So again, I searched for another explanation."

Reginald stood up and fixed his shirt, never breaking eye contact with Bob. "So, I realized it was because you had the notion that I would not follow through. So...here we are. I have your parents in my custody. And now I'll show you that I follow through with my threats." He then turned to Charlie and Ned. "Charles. Edward. I apologize for not extending to you both a similar warning before exacting punishment, but I'm sure you understood the risks of interfering with my business."

Bob failed to notice the horde of thugs that surrounded them, closing in like an encroaching tide. They were quiet as church mice as Reginald spoke, but once he finished, their threatening whispers rang out, layering on each other until it drowned out the faint music from the bars or the honks of the boats sailing along the river. Reginald cleared his throat and cracked his knuckles, and they went silent.

"I have little interest in what you three have to say to explain your actions or thoughts about me. All I want to hear is that you will cease this nonsense and let this city's cuisine move into the future."

Sarah stood and looked at her buzzing phone. Before answering, she waved her hand and thugs snapped out from the crowd and covered Bob's, Charlie's, and Ned's mouths.

"Hi, Abagail," Sarah said, "so sorry for the delay. We decided to open the invitation to the Lorox's as well. Do you know them? Ezekiel and Leah?...Wonderful. We just really thought it would be great to have you both in the same place...Yes...Of course...We will be there as soon as we can. Alright, you just enjoy the wine with Nathan!" With a fake laugh, she hung up the phone, and the thugs let go of the superheroes.

Reginald grimaced, knowing he had won. "Now that you have been...reminded...of the situation. I'd like you to join me for a boat ride."

Reginald and Sarah escorted them, along with a handful of thugs, onto a large white luxury yacht. It had two levels, a mini pool on the lower one and a hot tub on the other. The yacht also had more amenities than any hotel Bob stayed at, ranging from the fluffiest robes hanging poolside, a golf tee to swing off into the water, and multiple bars.

As they climbed on, arms tied behind their backs, serving thugs stared them down as they set a dinner table or made smoothies. These serving thugs looked like they were from a five-star restaurant but kept the normal spike hair, facial piercings, and tattoos. They wore black and white tuxedos and polished, black dress shoes.

Reginald slowly turned on his heel and crossed his arms. He looked down on the three superheroes with such condescension, it gave confidence to his nearby thugs.

"This is where we say our goodbyes. Ms. Crafterson and I are retiring to soak our feet before dinner with your parents at Still Rivers. I would normally say it was a pleasure to know you, but there is no sense in lying to someone before their departure from this world. So, I will just say farewell."

"I'm sure your parents will cry when we explain the news," Sarah said. "They won't mourn for long before they join you." She smiled.

Ned growled and squeezed his fists. Before he could respond, Charlie said, "Why kill them? Why not just have the dinner and leave them alone?"

Sarah looked confused for a moment like she received an obvious question from a child and was debating on how to respond. After a moment, she glanced at Reginald, who smirked, then turned to the three heroes.

"You three have been a thorn in our side. Within the past hour alone, I have received numerous reports from my associates of a rebellion among my once loyal customers. Those ungrateful worms smash my products and stain my reputation! I cannot have that. Rebellion must be dealt with and my reputation restored. I do not want the people of this city thinking I am a man to be trifled with." He stared a Bob for a moment. "So, now I will deal with your mistakes. Swiftly. I will hang your costumes on the side of my warehouse. Then, I will personally deliver to each ungrateful worm a box of broken spatulas, shattered wine bottles and crushed sandwiches. Finally, as I deliver the box, I will tell the story of your families' end. No message is clearer than ending an entire family. Then maybe I will finally have peace in this city. That's all I ever wanted. Peace."

Reginald exhaled and walked up to Ned so they only stood a couple of inches apart. He stared down at Ned and grinned. Charlie tried to lunge forward, but a couple of thugs held him back. Reginald snickered and said, "Does that answer your question, Mr. Lorox?"

Ned bit his tongue but stared back with enough animosity to convey his message.

"Excellent." Reginald said.

Bob stuck his tongue out at them right as Reginald and Sarah turned around. He snapped it back into his mouth when Reginald raised a finger, stopped, and turned back to them.

"Oh, and please remove all of your gear. Now. I rather dislike surprises so close to dinner time and want to preclude you from having any surprising or foolish inclinations. My associates will move it for safe keeping."

The three stripped off their gear. Charlie wore gym shorts and an undershirt, but Bob and Ned were stuck in their underwear. For a moment, he noticed Sarah smirking as she examined Bob. He took a step backward and tried to cover his groin area. Sarah's gaze moved up to meet his eyes, then she turned away.

Reginald respectfully nodded. "Thank you for your cooperation. Farewell." He turned to the escort and said, "Once we reach a sufficient depth, please terminate them and dispose of their bodies. I expect it to be done before we arrive."

Reginald and Sarah disappeared deeper into the boat while the escort shoved the superheroes into a living room and slammed the door shut, which locked with a decisive click.

The nausea washed over Bob, who regretted not putting his mask back on. All he could feel was the yacht moving underneath him, like he was standing on a platform resting on a ball as he spun quickly. His stomach showed its disapproval of the situation.

He took heavy and careful steps to the white button couch and slid onto it ever so slowly. If his stomach barely shifted, maybe it wouldn't hate him as much and he would be able to survive this boat ride with no medicine or glasses. But then it dawned on him. He was not going to survive this boat ride. He gently leaned back, closed his eyes, and breathed deeply. His heart raced, his breaths were shallow and his muscles pulsed with adrenaline. Here he was. Sitting on a boat. About to throw up on his way to be disposed of. "Motion medicine. Please."

"Damn it, Bob. Where's your mask?" Charlie said. Bob heard him approach and gestured for him to stop.

"Too late for mask. Need drugs. Ginger ale. Alka Seltzer."

"Well, you're out of luck."

"Don't be a dick, Charlie. I'll ask. Reginald's mad, but maybe his thugs will cut us some slack," Ned said. He knocked on the locked door. "Hey, do you mind getting us something for my friend's stomach? He doesn't do well on boats." There was no response. Ned tried a couple more times, but after not getting a response, he said, "Sorry, Bob. The yacht club shouldn't be too far from here."

With eyes shut tightly, Bob heard Ned and Charlie walk away from the door. Ned joined Charlie on the opposite side of the room. They mumbled to each other. It sounded like they were planning something. The discussion went back and forth. Both of them spoke in conceding and disputing tones like a tennis match.

Oh, no. Moving. Bob felt ill again as the yacht moved away from the docks out onto the massive river surrounding Central City.

Once he felt a little better about twenty minutes later, he wondered why he couldn't hear them talking anymore. He lifted his head up slightly to see. Charlie was cutting off something on Ned. No. He was sawing through the ropes around their wrists. Part of him was relieved they had a plan. The larger part hated the idea of moving.

Bob prayed they would take long enough for them to dock and get off the boat. Maybe a few more minutes so Bob could recover. That would be ideal.

"Bob," Ned said quietly in his ear. "We need you to roll over. Yup, just like that on your stomach. We're really sorry, but we're not giving up."

Bob wasn't giving up either. He was just hoping for better conditions. With his eyes shut tightly and breathing steady, he followed Ned's instructions.

"Okay. All set," Ned said. He patted Bob on the back and walked away.

Charlie approached. As he cut the bindings from Bob's wrists, he whispered. "Sorry about this, Bob, but this is the best way you can help." Then Charlie yelled.

"Hey! Bob's vomiting all over the carpet! Oh, God! It's on the painting of Nathan and Reginald! The one he doesn't shut up about." That last part was frighteningly specific.

"Sorry about what? What do you mean I'm vomiting." Bob whispered back. Then it dawned on him. "Wait, no! Please! No!" His voice was quiet but seething.

Charlie gripped his shoulders then shook him violently. When Bob went to say stop, words didn't exit his mouth. Instead, it was a hot, acidic stream of whatever was in his stomach.

"Oh, it's so bad! It's going to ruin this boat!" Ned said. "Reginald loves this room, too! He's gonna kill whoever let this happen."

The door swung open, and four thugs burst in. They gasped.

"Oh, God! What's that smell," one said.

"What were they talking about. The painting's fine," another said.

Bob was too distracted from vomiting and dry heaving to watch, but he heard tussling.

Thwack! Heavy metallic whacks reverberated around the room as if Ned and Charlie hit someone with a metal rod.

"Got one!" Charlie said. Ned said the same.

Then, the sounds turned more aggressive. The combatants grunted. The sound of punches whooshed and smacked. Furniture tumbled over. Glass broke. Charlie and Ned cursed through their teeth between landing hits and being hit back. One thug called for help, but another whack silenced him. Then, a thud as another body hit the floor. The room became quiet after the last thug hit the floor.

"I..." Bob said. "Hate you. So much. Charlie." Bob stood up and wiped his vomit off with a throw pillow. He couldn't tell if the boat had stopped. His mind was still too jumbled from Charlie's dick move of forcing Bob to vomit.

"You'll get over it," Charlie said. "Now, come on. We gotta get our stuff."

"We don't have much time" Ned said. "The yacht club is always bragging about how close they are to the city. Oh god. Bob, you reek. I'm gonna be sick." He quickly exited the room.

Charlie gave a judging look, like it was Bob's fault. Bob responded with an impatient stare back. He hoped Charlie made a comment, so he could unleash the verbal ammo he had prepared. Instead, Charlie stayed quiet and left the room. Bob did the same.

Charlie took the lead as they snuck around the halls. Ned lagged behind to help Bob stand. Bob still felt woozy and disgusting though not as bad as when they first took off. However, he was in no shape to do anything else besides walk.

Ahead, Charlie moved with military efficiency. Charlie's last job was an actor/director for spy thrillers and those skills transferred to this situation very well. He made hand gestures, which Ned understood immediately. Ned whispered the translations to Bob.

"Stop," Ned said.

A couple of thugs strolled by, snacking on some Raghu product.

"Down."

They snuck past a counter with thugs on the other side.

"Cover."

Ned and Bob dashed inside an open door as fast as they could.

"Two hostiles."

Charlie hid in another room, leaving the door slightly ajar. Three thugs walked by. Charlie's eye glared through the crack between the inner frame and door, watching them. Bob recognized the same predatory look in Reginald and Sarah. Charlie vanished deeper into the room. The thugs passed. Armed only with a red throw pillow he pilfered from the room, Charlie slipped out. He moved so silently it was like he erased all sound in the hallway.

With his body low, he lunged at the left most thug. Charlie slammed the thug's head into the sheetrock with so much force, the man collapsed. Before the right most thug screamed, Charlie smothered her face with the pillow held in his left hand. He slammed his fist into her stomach, forcing her to exhale. With the air out of her body, he snapped the pillow away and into the last standing thug, causing him to flinch.

The female thug toppled over, gasping for air. Charlie chopped at the back of her neck. She dropped to the ground. The last guard drew his gun, slightly delayed from the pillow attack. Charlie spun around on his heel, smacked the guard's elbow pit, forcing the guard's arm to collapse. Charlie pressed the momentum and twisted the gun directly at the guard's face.

"Don't pull it. Don't be stupid," Charlie said with the same gravelly voice from his acting days.

The guard looked horrified. Bob did as well. Charlie was brutal when he wanted to be. He probably could be a top spy in real life if he tried.

"Good boy," Charlie said, slowly unraveling the thug's fingers from the gun's grip. The thug trembled under the weight of Charlie's glare. Before anyone realized, Charlie released the magazine and slyly kicked the ammo into the room where Bob hid. Charlie then pointed to the room he came from.

"Bring your friends in there. Lock the door. You fucking say anything. I come back," he said.

The thug nodded and quietly obeyed. Right before the last thug locked himself away, Charlie held the door open.

"Where's our stuff," he said.

"B-b-bottom level. Storage."

Charlie just smiled and let the thug close the door, which instantly clicked locked. Charlie looked back to where Bob and Charlie hid and gestured something. Ned translated.

"Follow."

They continued through the yacht. Charlie occasionally dispatched guards with the same deadly efficiency he showed before. There was no sign of Reginald or Sarah. Bob briefly wondered how large this yacht was that they hadn't been alerted to Bob, Ned and Charlie's escape.

At one point, while Charlie was several feet ahead, Bob whispered to Ned.

"Who's this version of Charlie?"

After a moment, Ned replied, "The Charlie that isn't pretending to be a superhero."

Bob gulped. Charlie went from "Spatchy Spatch" to bashing people's heads into walls. He didn't kill anyone, but it looked like he came very close.

"It's hard to be a hero," Ned said. "Especially for Charlie. He puts a lot of pressure on himself. The costume restrains him. Without it, he's just himself."

They headed down an ornate staircase that led to a more industrial part of the boat. As they descended, Bob felt the boat still and the engine quiet down. They had stopped and did not have much more time.

The elegant beige walls turned into textured, white metal. The wood floors were replaced by cheap checkered plastic. A couple steel bulkhead doors down, they found the storage room and inside was their gear.

Charlie closed the door behind them right as Bob made it inside.

"Good work," he said. "Let's move quick. Our parents need saving."

Ned raised an eyebrow to Bob as if to ask if Bob could stand on his own. Bob nodded back and mouthed, *thanks.* While Ned focused on reequipping his gear, Bob tiptoed over to Charlie.

"Hey, you okay over there?"

Charlie glanced at Bob. For a second, he was the violent Charlie from before, the image of unattached and calculated brutality. Then, the Charlie Bob knew came back.

"Hey, yeah. Are you? Looks like you're feeling a bit better."

Bob awkwardly knocked on the wall, more focused on trying to suppress his fear of evil Charlie.

"Oh, me? Yeah. *Pshhh.* Totally cool. I just, you know, saw you doing the knocking-people-out thing. Didn't seem like you. Like the normal you. But you know if you're cool, then, we're cool. But also if you're not cool, you know, you can like talk to me and stuff. It's important to be like open and honest. But also, it's okay to like have secrets and stuff. I respect you either way."

"Thanks, Bob."

Bob bit his lip. He did his rambling thing again. With one last uncomfortable thumbs-up, he turned back to putting on his gear. He noticed Ned, smothering a laugh in the corner. Charlie didn't seem to notice since his attention was fully on his super elaborate and intricate costume. It had so many parts.

After taking back their confiscated equipment, they retraced their path and exited the yacht, emerging at the top level with the perfect view of the Still Rivers yacht club. At night, Still Rivers was strange, a bright beacon surrounded by darkness. There wasn't much around the club for miles, and the passing road didn't have many streetlights.

The lobby's lights were still on, allowing them to see inside through the French door entrances and the large windows lining the riverside of the building on the first floor of the yacht club. The banquet hall on the second floor, with similar large windows, was illuminated as well. However, dark red luxurious curtains blocked them from seeing inside. Bob could still glean silhouettes moving about the banquet hall, but they were too far away to see any more than that. The building's two decks stacked on top of each other, connected by an outdoor staircase, were mostly unlit, barely visible under the ambient light and the moon shining in the sky. Even the surrounding landscaping and grounds along the riverside were poorly lit.

Between them and the Still Rivers building, dull orange light washed over the faded wooden planks forming the dock. Any orange light that didn't settle on the wood disappeared in the void of black water below. The water sloshed around like it was trying to leap up and devour anyone who fell into its depths. Even the boats were intimidating. The hulls of the other yachts croaked as they slid against dock bumpers. Dozens of yacht flags flapped in the steady winds, sounding like claps.

They were on the largest boat, but the others were still skyscrapers in their own rights. Bob spotted his parents' yacht, which was much smaller, on the far-left side of the docks. Seeing their yacht seemed to be the only normal part of tonight and provided a bit of comfort. However, that ended the moment he remembered they were probably inside with Reginald in his massive, dangerous grasp.

Charlie pulled Bob down beneath the yacht's railings.

He whispered, "Reginald's walking out. When he's back inside, he'll let his guard down. Then we —" Charlie punched the palm of his hand to emphasize his meaning.

Bob nodded in agreement and slipped on his mask.

"Okay, let's move," Charlie said.

Ned took the lead, crouching over while he walked toward the stairs that led to the yacht's boarding level. He hid beneath the handrails of Reginald's yacht. Bob slipped when he tried to follow. His knee banged against the railing, sending a rattling noise into the relatively quiet night.

Reginald's head whipped to Bob's direction, and he stared. Even though Reginald was at least a hundred yards away, Bob felt like Reginald was gazing into his soul. However, Bob couldn't make out the details on Reginald's face, so he couldn't see any recognition or reaction. After an eternity of Bob holding his breath and sweating, Reginald finally walked back toward the yacht club building with his squad of ten thugs.

Ned visibly relaxed and kept going ahead, Bob next and Charlie in the rear. By the time they made it to the docks, one thug closed the doors to the lobby behind Reginald. The thug stayed on the deck, looking out onto the water with a cigarette in her hand. A tiny orange dot at the tip of the cigarette brightened, then dimmed as the thug exhaled a cloud of smoke. Post exhale, the thug concentrated on her phone.

Still Rivers' docks formed five aisles that all ended at one long perpendicular platform, making it look like a giant comb. Every few feet was a water hose. Bob used one of them to wash off his uniform with ice cold water. The water felt like knives dragging against his skin, but he held back complaints and suffered the shivering in silence. Charlie and Ned watched from behind some crates and laughed.

They continued along the dock, diving behind crates, barrels, and posts. Suddenly, the sentinel thug glanced up from her phone. The group turned still as stone. It was a half-present survey, but in their superhero outfits, Ned, Bob, and Charlie would have stood out. Charlie signaled for them to gather up behind cover and whispered.

"We need to take her out," Charlie said. "If I get any closer, she's gonna hear my armor."

"Told you not to make actual armor," Ned said, rolling his eyes.

"How the hell was I supposed know that we'd be doing stealth ops."

"Because I—"

"Hi, um," Bob said, slowly moving his hands up then down to calm down tensions. "Ned and I can handle the lady. I'm starting to feel better you know after the whole boat incident, and I'm just ready to, you know, do my part and stuff."

"I can't leave you two to do this. I'm the leader," Charlie said. Ned cranked his head back in shock. Before he could reply, Bob spoke first.

"If you go, we lose the element of surprise," Bob said.

"Then screw it, let's shock them," Charlie said. "Bob, you have grenades right. Hurl it onto the deck, we take the guy out, strike in the chaos."

"No," Ned said. "Our parents are still in there. We can't go in crazy. Reginald and Sarah have leverage. They think we are dead. Our parents are only alive as long as they continue to think we are dead."

Bob agreed. Reginald clearly didn't expect to see them again based on the farewell and instructions to the thug that took their things. The confidence he exuded after getting off the boat only proved he thought they were dead. Villains were only that confident after they won.

"That's stupid," Charlie said. "I'm the one who actually did this for a living."

Bob raised an eyebrow, wondering what Charlie was talking about. They had all been actors for the same TV show, though Charlie, Ned and Lila had more experience than him. It was just odd phrasing. Ned seemed to have noticed his confusion.

"We were *both* actors, Charlie. Don't forget Bob's here too and was also an *actor*, who did stunts."

Charlie bit his lip but nodded. Bob jumped in.

"I agree with Ned. I'm sorry, but my parents are in danger too and I'd feel better being quiet."

"Whatever. When this goes sideways, I'm going in hot."

Once they got to the end of the wooden dock, Charlie hung back. Bob and Ned moved onto dry land. Bob and his stomach appreciated no longer having the wooden planks slightly shifting under his weight.

Roughly twenty yards ahead along a path of white stone pavers was an opulent, white deck made of a composite wood. The deck buttressed up the building and had French glass doors leading into the lobby. The building's deck also had three small stairs leading up to it, one in the center and one on each side. Short, bristly grass, still barely alive from the winter, filled the space between the paths connecting the deck and the docks. The area between the yacht club and the water was poorly lit.

Bob went left. Ned went right. Bob crept along the pavers toward the building, so carefully he couldn't even hear his own footsteps. He held some crostini throwing stars in his hand, ready to strike. They would be silent and effective. The bread that composed the throwing stars was so stale it would feel like a baseball colliding with the side of your head.

Bob squatted as he reached the top of the left stairs, keeping his body under the deck's flooring to avoid being seen. Across the way, he could see Ned, who counted down with his fingers. Three. Two. One. Bob hurled the crostini throwing star.

Thwmp. The crostini throwing star slammed the thug's temple, instantly knocking her out. Right before the body crashed to the floor, Ned slid underneath and caught it. He dragged the body off the deck and tucked the unconscious thug underneath the stairs. Now that the sentinel was taken down, Charlie caught up since his clanky armor was not observable anymore. Once he caught up, he tied up the thug.

With the coast temporarily clear, Bob peaked his head inside and saw there were a few thugs strolling around inside of the Still Rivers lobby.

The lobby was a giant square. Each corner of the room had white columns with seagulls, masts, sails, and other nautical themed carvings climbing up each side, which combined with the light blue walls to give the guests an oceanic feeling. Straight ahead was the main entrance, and to the immediate left was the check-in desk, built out of a glossy deep brown stone with black flecks randomly scattered about. The desk faced a spiral staircase tucked into the corner that led to the banquet room above.

A couple of thugs stood by the check-in desk and the others roamed about or sat on the beige couches and uphol-stered chairs. They didn't really seem concerned.

Suddenly, the thugs all snapped to attention and stood up. Their eyes focused on Reginald coming down the stair-case. He descended one stair at a time and savored each step. Reginald apathetically looked over the lobby and at each one of his thugs. He stopped at the last step and started speaking.

"Eyes on Reginald. He's saying something," Bob said. He closed his eyes, hoping he could better focus and hear something through the glass. No luck. The glass doors muffled the sound too much. The volume of whatever Reginald said was steady, so it didn't sound like he was angry.

"What is it?" Ned asked.

Charlie lifted his mask and said, "What about our parents?"

Bob inched forward from the group's hiding spot. His heart sped up. Any benefit to moving closer to the glass doors was drowned out by his heavier breathing and pounding heart. He pulled back, defeated, and shook his head. "I'm sorry, guys. I can't hear any specifics."

"Damn it," Charlie said. "We can't waste any time. Ned and I will distract. We're in better shape and can handle fighting the thugs and Reginald. You take the back stairs to the upper deck while they're distracted and —"

One of the sliding doors whooshed open, and Reginald stepped out, the deck shaking under his weight.

"Where's Sharon?" he said, staring out into the night. Someone inside replied.

"She was out there a couple of minutes ago," he said.

"That's irrelevant. She's not here now. I don't care where she was a couple of minutes ago. If I cared, I would have asked!" Reginald stepped back inside and slammed the sliding doors shut, cracking the glass. Other people spoke, but Reginald's thunderous voice boomed even through the closed doors.

"Holy shit," Bob said as he released his breath. Instinctually, he had clenched every part of his body in a desperate attempt to make himself smaller and pressed up against the siding of the main building. Even after releasing his breath, none of his muscles relaxed. His heart still felt like it was going to leap out of his throat. "He's a scary dude."

Ned nodded. "When I was a kid, he caught me running around the club." He shuddered. "I didn't run around again."

"He's a jerk," Charlie said. "He's nothing but a big bully who throws his weight around. They fall down just the same. Bob, go. We'll hold them for as long as we can."

Bob retreated toward the water and took the long way outside the staircase that led to the upper deck, never stepping out of the shadows. His heart pounded against his already sore ribs. He wasn't nearly as stealthy as he would've liked. He was on extraction and didn't have a lot of time. He couldn't afford it. He had to take risks.

Whoosh! Bang! Once Bob was out of their sight, Ned and Charlie hurled open the lobby's sliding doors, which bashed into the frame. There was loud, angry shouting by the thugs and his friends as they crossed into the yacht club's lobby. Suddenly, his lack of stealth didn't seem to matter.

Ned and Charlie closed the doors behind themselves. The night was quieter. Bob still heard the chaos. He pictured all the vases and decorations smashing against the floor, the furniture breaking or exploding against the wall in a splinter storm. He had the easy job, which normally he'd feel guilty about, but after Charlie made him throw up on the boat, he didn't feel as bad.

He reached Still Rivers' top deck. He glanced backward and looked at Central City in the distance, shining brightly. Even the massive river that flowed past the yacht club was peaceful. Bob hoped all the people they had helped were able to protect their stores and culinary traditions.

Hearing Ned and Charlie yell snapped him back to focus. No matter what they'd done so far, it would all be meaningless if Reginald and Sarah went free. Bob turned away from the water and headed toward to the glass door leading inside the building's second floor. He peeked through. There were tables and chairs set up normally. The ceilings were white with exposed wooden beams that connected to white columns like the ones in the lobby. The walls were a light purple and the floors a sandstone. The tables were shoved up against the walls except for one large one in the center. Unfortunately, he saw people but couldn't figure out who was sitting at it. Then his heart stopped.

Reginald shot into view. The mountain of a man thundered past him and headed downstairs. Once he was out of sight, Bob peeked into the room. The only people inside were the Loroxes. So, Bob sprinted into the banquet hall. Charlie and Ned were outnumbered and with Reginald entering the fight, time was running out.

"Mr. and Mrs. Lorox," he said. Bob ran over as Ned's and Charlie's parents ran to him. They hugged though Bob was distracted by the two unused place settings with name tags for his parents.

"Where are our boys?" Mrs. Lorox said, holding Bob at arm's length.

"They're downstairs, holding off Reginald and his gang. Once we're all out, we can escape," Bob said. Mr. Lorox nodded, took his wife's hand, and escorted her out through the back door. Bob caught Mrs. Lorox's trailing arm.

"What about my parents?" He stopped breathing.

Mrs. Lorox stared at him, crestfallen.

"I'm sorry, Bob. I don't know. We got here, and they were missing. We haven't seen them."

Bob let go. His whole body went limp, and he stared at the floor. While he looked absent, his mind was very much racing. He imagined running outside, down the deck stairs, back to the dock and to the river's edge. He imagined diving into the water and to the bottom of the water where he pictured his parents lying in some horribly gruesome way. All of it was because he wanted to help people. He was selfish and wanted something exciting. He had an awesome girlfriend, supportive parents, great friends, and an okay job. He risked it all. What if he was just happy with what he had? What if he had a spine and stood up to Reginald? What if he—

Mr. Lorox shook him from his thoughts. "Hey, Bob. I'm sure they're okay, but we won't be if we stay here."

Bob pointed absently to the back door. He wasn't going to run. Not this time. After losing so much, he wouldn't be the guy who hid from customers. He'd be brave. Emrys said he wasn't manager ready, but Bob would show him. Thinking back, Reginald was just one pissed off, passive aggressive, entitled customer, and Bob was the god damn manager.

"Go. I'll be fine."

"I really don't think you will be." Mr. Lorox laughed uncomfortably. "Please. Don't do anything stupid. They're okay, and I don't want to explain that they lost their son because he went and did something stupid."

Bob glared into Mr. Lorox's eyes. "Go." Bob turned and dashed down the stairs.

Chapter Eleven

The lobby was decimated. The papers on the check-in desk were strewn about, covering the floor. There was a crack running through the desk's granite counter, likely caused by the shattered, metal stanchion on top of it. The furniture and small tables were thrown about. Lamps, chairs, and planters protruded from the walls like strange abstract art.

Then he saw Reginald, standing in the center of the room, his hair frazzled, and Hawaiian shirt ripped. The mountain of a man breathed heavily with his back to Bob. The couple of remaining thugs stared at the same thing as Reginald, equally run down and out of breath. Bob peered past them to see Charlie and Ned, their masks ripped off and bloodied. They were on their knees, blood streaming down from their mouths. Anger swelled in Bob's chest.

"Reginald!" His chest throbbed. It wasn't from fear this time. Bob wanted to fight. He wanted Reginald to talk down to him and throw the first swing. He wanted to punch Reginald once, then again, then again.

Reginald slowly faced the last standing hero. He stared at Bob dispassionately as if destroying Bob was in the ordinary course of business. Once Bob would have trembled under Reginald's sight, but after working retail at Merlin's Warehouse, fighting to save food, having his home attacked, losing his parents, and staring at his wounded friends Reginald was not as scary. He was just a big customer for Bob to handle.

Reginald's thugs moved forward, but halted as Reginald raised a hand. They stopped in their tracks. With a slightly turned head, he addressed his thugs.

"I will handle this. Make sure our other guests do not move." Reginald turned back to Bob. "Mr. Johnson, I wondered if I would have to search for you, but again, you surprise me. How foolish to expect a fool not to fool. Come. Let us end this."

"Screw you."

Bob took a breath. The air raced through his lungs. His heart beat quickly. This was it. He swiftly drew his katana, the blade whistling against the sheath. Charlie and Ned yelled for Bob to flee, but that wasn't an option for him. Bob raised the blade and squeezed the grip.

With his sword overhead, Bob leaped at Reginald. Time slowed as Bob aimed his blow directly at Reginald's head. The edge howled as he brought it down. Charlie and Ned continued crying out, but Bob couldn't hear it over the adrenaline pumping through his veins.

The obedient thugs stood still as statues. Reginald retreated a step and side stepped. He swatted the sword aside with his massive hand. Bob stumbled forward, carried by the momentum of his missed slash.

Reginald's eyes locked with his. The man looked bored. He unemotionally reached for Bob. Before Bob could recover, Reginald's powerful grip clenched on the back of his neck. He lifted Bob into the air. Bob's feet left the ground and thrashed about, trying to kick Reginald or find purchase to escape. He failed.

"How could someone as stupid as you disrupt my empire? Clearly the other two were the brains."

He hurled Bob over the check-in counter. Bob sailed through the air and collided into a painting hanging on the wall. As gravity slammed him into the floor, the painting fell on top of him. Then, a rack of keys toppled onto him, which hurt a lot more. He coughed. No blood, which was a welcomed surprise. Unfortunately, he didn't have long to appreciate it.

"Disappointing. Get him." Reginald waved a dismissive hand, like the breath wasn't worth his time.

Bob groaned and pushed himself to his feet. He lost his sword but still had a few more crostini throwing stars and a marinara grenade at his waist. Then the thugs were on him.

He threw his body against the wall to avoid a metal pipe being swung by a thug. The wielder followed up with a horizontal swing. Bob ducked below the pipe. The thug swung with so much force that the displaced air tickled Bob's head. The pipe missed and wedged itself into the wall. Taking advantage of the distraction, Bob launched himself up with a fist positioned right below the thug's jaw. He thrust. His fist, like a spear tip, crushed the thug's jaw. The thug toppled backward. Bob took a breath and stood up to see—

Whack. Something slammed against Bob's chest, and he gasped. Another thug held the remnants of a table, the rest of which laid at Bob's feet. He leapt backward to avoid the second swing of the broken table. His spine smacked into the sharp corner of the check-in desk and sent a jolt down his leg. Bob pushed aside the pain and blasted his fist forward. He slammed his fist into the thug's jaw. There was a crunch of teeth shattering, and the thug's hands ran to his mouth. The thug howled.

Bob snagged one of the table legs at his feet and whacked the thug on the left ribs then returned with a back-swing that hit the thug on the other side. The thug winced and fled toward Reginald.

Reginald furiously glared at the thug, and the thug stopped in his tracks. Bob hurled the leg at the back of the thug's head, and he collapsed to the floor.

Bob looked around. Charlie and Ned were gone. Since the doors to the deck were open, they must've escaped. Reginald didn't react aside from seething at his thug's fleeing and the fact that Bob was still standing. He must not have noticed. Bob thought he saw Charlie's metal armor in the distance, and he sighed. Reginald bellowed. His condescending yet irritated laugh felt like it shook the building.

"You think there is a point to this? You all get away. Then what? I know where you all live. I know all of your credit card numbers. I have your friends' addresses and financial information. Leave the country? I don't care. There is no place in the entire world you can run from me. I. Will. End. You." Reginald had grown rabid, the lion within him craving violence. He paused a moment to compose himself. "So, how do you wish to proceed, Bob?"

Bob took a breath. It was just him and Reginald. Bob could feel all his old wounds opening. His legs trembled from exhaustion and breathing hurt. The motion sickness had passed, but now his head throbbed. Reginald looked tired but was in much better shape than Bob. Clearly the benefit of having an army of thugs to do your work.

Luckily, Charlie and Ned were gone. They made it out. They'd last the night, stop Reginald, and protect his friends, the city, the food. Bob enjoyed his short run as a superhero.

If only Emrys could see him now. Reginald was the ultimate retail nightmare and Bob stood up to him. Bob had the manager personality in him the whole time, just didn't discover it until now. It felt like the cheesy conclusion of those Hollywood block buster movies. Lila loved those. Too bad she was going to kick his ass when she saw all these injuries. He chuckled, which enraged Reginald.

"Now? At a time like this, you laugh!" Reginald's face turned red. Spit frothed and spray as he spoke. His tranquility was completely gone.

"Yeah. Lila would probably kill me for doing this even if I survived. Last time we talked"—Bob coughed out some blood, which blended into his suit rather well—"she said to be safe. I guess I didn't listen too well."

Reginald chuckled. His temper settled and he spoke with a generous warmth like they were two old friends. "A shame. I look forward to meeting her. I'll let her know your last thoughts were of her. She must be...very special."

"Yeah, I love her. I didn't get my chance to tell her. I will though." Bob returned to a fighting stance. "You want me to pass anything along to Nathan?"

Reginald did the same. "I'll tell him that I'll see him at home."

Bob sprinted forward. Reginald jabbed. Bob slipped under the boulder-like fist. He planted his right foot and hooked a fist at Reginald's rib cage. Reginald leaped backwards to evade Bob's swing. He spun on a heel and swung around his tree trunk leg. Bob raised his arms to block the blow, but it sent him reeling backward. He crashed into the wall, the sheetrock caving behind him. Bob rolled aside just in time to evade Reginald's fist, which smashed through the wall.

Reginald yanked out his fist, dust puffing from the

crater. Before Reginald could turn to face him, Bob stayed low and punched Reginald right below his ribs. After landing his blow, Bob noticed Reginald's knee screaming toward Bob's face. Bob narrowly dodged by throwing his weight backward and rolling.

Bob rolled onto his back to catch the pursuing Reginald's stomp. Bob's hands wrapped around the front of his shoe and the heel. He kicked Reginald's planted foot just above the ankle, forcing it to slide backwards and causing Reginald to lose his balance. Reginald collapsed to the floor like a boulder.

Bob crab-walked backwards and bumped into someone. He glanced up.

It was Rachel. She looked the same as when he fought her last, though much angrier.

"Hey, Bob," she said his name venomously. "I heard you were still alive, so I had to get my piece before Reginald ended you."

Bob scrambled away but bumped into another person, who chuckled. Bob recognized Purple Bo's voice.

"Me too," he said, shoving Bob prone. He seized Bob by an arm and leg. After spinning around a couple of times, Purple Bo threw him back toward the entrance. Bob's suit screeched as he slid against the floor. He flipped over to see Reginald standing over him, flanked by Rachel and Purple Bo. Reginald squatted down and frowned.

"Admirable," Reginald said. He grabbed Bob, who was out of energy, and threw him through the front doors and onto a porch. Bob rolled down the porch's wooden steps. He landed on the pebble roundabout that formed the Still Rivers driveway, kicking up a cloud of dust in the process. Small black lanterns rested on the ground, wrapping along the roundabout. They slightly illuminated the way, but their dimness made it feel like Bob was going to be a sacrifice. If not for the white, concrete awning supported by white ionic columns, the full moon above would shine down on him and truly complete the human sacrifice aesthetic.

Bob coughed. More blood decorated the pebbles beneath him. Bob pushed himself up.

Reginald stood underneath the porch light mounted in the awning in a way that, ironically, made him look angelic. Bob laughed. Something else ridiculous about this whole night.

Reginald smashed his fist through one of the porch's support pillars.

"Still! You laugh at me! How can you still fight? Still resist me?"

Bob pushed to his feet and chuckled again. "I wish I knew."

A cone of yellow light appeared, covering Bob and everyone on the porch. Then another cone appeared and another. Then they appeared in twos, threes, fours. There were so many lights, Bob forgot for a moment that it was night and the world should be dark. He turned around, but it was blinding. They were headlights from cars, vans, and motorcycles. Some of the vans had names, which Bob recognized as local restaurants. People poured out of the vehicles. They had to be responding to Moni's broadcast. He was lucky to be her friend.

When Bob turned back, Reginald looked different. He had something on his face that Bob had never seen before.

Fear.

"Bob! We will take it from here," someone said.

"Sergio?" Bob said. He raised his hand over his eyes to shield the light. It worked just enough for him to see Sergio walking toward him, armed with a rolling pin. Maria, his daughter, stood next to him with a metal serving spoon in each hand. An army of different store owners, chefs and culinary artisans followed quickly behind them, including Mr. Ross and Mr. Kwok.

"Yes, my friend," Sergio said. "Charlie told us where you were. We came as soon as we could. Now, you don't save the city alone. We save it together." He smiled and turned back to the army behind him. With his rolling pin held high, Sergio stared into the ominous and uncertain night and summoned all of his strength. To his allies, he roared, "Cocineros! Vamos!"

It was a stampede as they charged forward. The ground shook under the weight of the chefs, clerks, and owners as they galloped en masse directly at Reginald. They swept past Bob like a hurricane gale toward the club. A roar rang out in the night, a thick batter of cheers, chants, and metal pots, pans, and utensils banging together. Maria jogged forward and helped Bob to his feet.

"Glad you're okay. My dad doesn't shut up about you," she said, smiling.

"I'm glad I'm okay too. Pops also told me you were looking at Florida schools. You should—"

"Associates! Come here! Now!" Reginald's voice trembled.

Thugs, familiar and new, streamed out to meet the stampede. It looked like two roaring rivers slamming into each other in a chaotic mess. The shouting continued through the whacks, rings, and banging. Both sides cried out in success and hurt.

At first, it looked like the deluge was pushing Reginald back. But he quickly broke through and swatted people away like flies. After a few seconds, Sergio's allies began avoiding Reginald.

"Robert! I'm not done with you yet!"

"Right. Battle," Bob said. "We can talk later. I know lots of people who can give you advice about Florida. Good luck!"

Bob stood on his own as Maria ran to defend her family's business, leaving Bob and Reginald alone to settle their score. Before Bob could move, something held him back.

"We're here too, Bob," Charlie said. Ned clapped a supportive hand on Bob's shoulder.

The three stood against Reginald, whose fear was gone. He snorted, his chest heaved as he exhaled pure fiery anger, which steamed in the night air. Bob could hear his friends behind him, probably just as winded as he was and far more beaten up.

Charlie charged first. He attacked Reginald's right side. As Reginald turned to counter Charlie, Ned attacked his flank. Reginald deflected Charlie's blow and punched him square in the chest. However, Ned punched Reginald's back and kicked the back of his knee. Reginald roared and swung a titanic fist backward, and it clipped Ned, who spun off the hit. Ned was still recovering when Reginald swung at him again.

Ned's eyes went wide, realizing that a direct hit would be devastating. Right before Reginald hit Ned, Bob hurled a crostini throwing star at Reginald's fist. The crostini painfully collided into the bare fist. Reginald yelled and yanked his hand back. His eyes locked with Bob's eyes. Neither of them flinched.

Reginald bull rushed Bob with a lowered shoulder. Unfortunately, Bob didn't have the strength to dodge it. Bob planted his feet and extended his arms, ready to catch the blow. Once Reginald was close enough, Bob clasped onto his enemy's shoulders. The force was daunting. Bob slid backward. Staying on his feet required all his effort. The unrelenting Reginald kept pushing. Suddenly, Bob felt Reginald sneak one of his legs behind Bob's. With one more push, Bob lost his footing, and the two crashed to the pebble driveway.

As they went down, Bob wrapped his arm around Reginald's neck and held on in the tumble. Reginald kicked and screamed like a pinned bull as Bob struggled to hold on. Bob's stamina quickly faded, and Reginald broke free.

"You insolent worm!" Reginald bellowed as he rose to his feet. After grabbing Bob by the leg, he dragged him along the paved path. With Herculean strength, Reginald threw Bob into one of the roundabout's columns. Bob collided with a harsh crack when his shoulder clipped the column and the rest of his body kept flying.

"Argh!" Bob screamed in pain. It felt like throbbing lava oozed from his shoulder joint. Reginald charged again at Bob, but Charlie stepped in front and intercepted him. The two clashed like football players fighting to push the other back. Dust puffed into the air. The pebbles ground under their chopping feet.

Suddenly, Ned appeared behind Reginald. He undid his wine tube and lassoed it around Reginald's neck. With a powerful yank, Reginald gasped, and Ned pulled him down.

Ned slipped underneath Reginald, wrapped his legs around Reginald's thick neck and squeezed.

"Surrender!"

Ned undid his lasso and tossed it to Charlie, who tied Reginald's legs together. Reginald screamed so many things, so many threats, but it was pointless. Charlie and Ned held on.

Reginald's strength faded. His kicks and twists slowed

like a fish out of water for too long. His curses were quieter and less frequent.

Bob stood, saving his free hand to hold his shoulder, which seared with pain. Every breath hurt just as much and smelled like metal, probably from the blood that stained his upper lip. He looked straight ahead because his throbbing headache was worse when he tried to look to either side.

Standing over Reginald, Bob realized the man wasn't as intimidating. Reginald had a fire in his eyes still, but the rest of his body had given up.

"You. Lost," Bob said.

Reginald stayed silent.

"Bob," Charlie said. "Tie him up."

Bob looked around and couldn't find anything nearby. There was rope inside, but he had an uneasy feeling about going to get it. Their victory was too precarious. The fighting between Central City's culinary champions and the thugs also seemed like it ended. Bob felt that the moment he stepped into the lobby, the thugs were going to attack, and they'd lose the battle. However, he couldn't be afraid. Bob had a job to do. He also had to learn to rely on his allies to help him out. Another lesson he was excited to tell his boss about.

"Bob!" Charlie said.

"There's rope inside," Bob said. He slowly climbed the stairs then cautiously entered the lobby.

Inside, the fighting had concluded. Unconscious or semi-conscious people laid across the floor or draped over the furniture. There were groans of pain. The walls were covered in ketchup, mustard, marinara, mayonnaise and several other sauces Bob could not identify. Broken utensils, dented pots and contorted pans scattered across the floor, effectively filling any space between people.

Then he heard a shout coming from the deck. He limped out as fast as he could.

It was Sergio. He was on the deck looking out at Sarah, who stood on the docks and held a dazed Maria. Maria was on her feet, but looked so wobbly that with one shove, Sarah could send her into the river. The river water slapped against the retaining wall and splashed up, eager to grab hold of Maria. All around them, the brawling continued as the thugs fought the chefs and cooks trying to save Maria.

"Fine!" Sergio said. "I will buy it. I'll buy all your terrible products. Just give me back my daughter."

"Our products aren't terrible," Sarah said. "You just don't see their benefit. Yet!" She shook Maria as a terrible reminder of her anger and the leverage Sarah had over the situation.

"Sarah!" Bob cried out then winced from the throat ache. He lowered his voice. "Reginald is done. We beat him. We don't have to do this anymore."

Her composure cracked, but she quickly restored it. "Reginald is never done. He always has a plan."

Bob slowly approached; one hand raised in surrender. He didn't have a plan, but at least he knew his objective. He had to get Sarah to accidentally let go of Maria, so he could save her. He was out of crostini throwing shards. He no longer had his sword and only one working shoulder. What was left?

His mind focused on the grenade hanging from his belt. He remembered a trick his parents would play on him. People instinctually caught something thrown at them or flinched. Either way, it would give Bob and Sergio the seconds they needed to save Maria. However, he couldn't let on that he was going to use it. The key was surprising her. Sarah was savvy and would spot his movement from a mile away. He needed help. Bob kept walking forward to the deck's center stairs, past Sergio, and stopped after going down the first step.

"Fine. Reginald has a plan," Bob said, hands raised, and slowly continued down another step. "You really think it involves hurting a young girl? You think he wouldn't *belt* out when he heard what you did?" After saying the words, Bob realized that Reginald might harm a child to get what he wanted. It didn't matter though since he only wanted to convey his true message to Sergio. He needed Sergio to grab the grenade.

Bob wanted to look back at Sergio to see if he realized, but he was still scared of Sarah catching on. After a moment, Sarah raised an eyebrow.

"Why did you say belt weird?"

"I like puns," Bob said.

"Really, Bob? You want to joke like this?" Sergio said. "Maria is in danger!"

"Sergio, shut up and *hang* on." Once again, hoping Sergio caught the translation. There was only one thing hanging from his belt and Sergio was a bright guy.

"Don't you dare tell me to shut up!"

Bob felt a push that sent him flying to the ground. Luckily, he landed on the grass and not the pavers.

"What was that for?" Bob said. He rolled onto his back, and he smiled. The grenade was gone. Sergio must've caught the Bob's hidden message and slyly knocked it off.

"It was for telling me to shut up!"

"Both of you! Enough! I'm the one in charge," Sarah said.

Clink. Clink. Clink. Clink. All eyes snapped to the marinara grenade rolling down the steps. Then it rolled along the pavers.

"What is that? Robert, is that one of your stupid tools?" Sarah said. "Get it away from me!"

"Fine! I'll get it," Bob said. Getting up from the ground with one arm was incredibly difficult. Sergio tried to help him up, but Sarah hissed and told Sergio to stop. Bob eventually stood up and grabbed the grenade. "Now what do you want me to do?"

"Give it to me," she said. "Reginald might find it useful."

"Wait, what? You just said to get it away from you. Now you want it."

"Yes!"

"So don't get it away from you. You now want it."

"Yes, you idiot. Give me it!"

Bob nodded and walked toward her with the hand holding the grenade extended.

"Don't give it to her!" Sergio said.

Bob walked forward. He stared into Sarah's eyes. Bob's focus was so intense he did not notice that all the thugs and chefs had stopped fighting. They watched in worried anticipation to see how this would end.

Bob searched Sarah's eyes for any recognition and suspicion. She was an unflinching steel trap. Did she know something was going on? Worse, did she know and have her own plan to counter it already and Bob was walking into it? Sarah was Reginald's second in command, a threat in her own right.

A few feet separated them. Bob spotted sweat on her brow. She was nervous. It might work.

She extended a hand to take the grenade from Bob. It was going to work.

"Catch." Bob tossed the grenade up. Sarah suddenly forgot she was holding Maria and reached forward for the grenade with two hands. Sergio barreled down the wooden stairs, his feet sounding like jackhammers, but he wasn't going to make it. The other people on Bob's side weren't going to make it. No one was going to make it. Only Bob was close enough. He had to be a superhero.

Bob leaped forward to the falling Maria, who looked peaceful as she fell toward the black water. Her arms extended like she was unconsciously asking to be saved.

Bob grabbed her wrist and yanked, propelling her to fall onto land. Unfortunately, Bob's movement carried him forward, and he fell into the water.

Splash. Air bubbles ran to the surface of the water. Bob could hear the bubbles rumbling by, which drowned out people yelling from above the water. Things eventually got quiet. Things also got cold as the water seeped through his costume and soaked the fabric. It felt like an ice blanket was covering him. It was heavy too. His bad shoulder was useless, and he couldn't fix his direction with his remaining limbs. So, Bob just held his breath and stared up at the distorted moon above him through the water. The image shook and wobbled as the water's surface settled as Bob sank deeper into the blackness.

Chapter Twelve

Bob stared up at the moon growing smaller and smaller, like he was walking back from light at the edge of a tunnel. Then something blocked the image of the white circle. It was a black shadow. It grew and grew. Then water above him trembled. The shadow got closer, grabbed Bob's wrist, and pulled. The shadow swung underneath him and pushed him up.

Bob breached the surface and gasped. It felt so good to breathe that Bob didn't care that it hurt. The shadow breached and Bob turned around.

Charlie smiled. "We aren't done with you yet," he said. Ned was up on the dock with Sergio, both with one arm extended. The two hoisted Bob out of the water. Maria wrapped Bob in a warm, soft blanket. It was immediately soaked, but it provided a thin shield against the chilly bites of the wind.

Bob looked around and didn't see anyone else outside. It was also quiet again. He didn't hear fists hitting faces or gasps as people had the wind knocked out of them.

"Let's get you inside," Sergio said. He and Ned slipped

under Bob's shoulders and supported him standing up. The three then hobbled toward the lobby. Charlie and Marie followed. Bob's teeth chattered the entire way.

After carefully traversing the stairs, Bob could see inside the lobby. The heavenly warmth oozed out through the open doors. As he continued looking inside, he realized that the fighting had stopped. The chefs, clerks, and owners peacefully stood next to the thugs. Some were even talking to each other. Then a thug spotted Bob.

"It's him! He's back!" the thug said.

Bob's heart was still racing from him almost drowning. Then it came to a stop so fast Bob thought it was going to burst through his chest. They were going to beat him up and free Reginald and keep fighting and he couldn't stop them, and Marie was in danger again and—

Clap. Clap. One by one, everyone in the lobby stopped talking and started clapping. They whistled! They cheered! They focused on him! Bob began sweating. Even though he was freezing, it was a lot of attention. He wondered what he should do. Should he yell thank you? Probably not since his throat was still burning. Should he raise a fist? Also, no because he would likely lose balance and topple to the floor. Instead, he just stood and stared at everyone. Not realizing his jaw had dropped and his mouth hung open, Bob scoured his mind for something to say. They seemed to notice since they began to look as uncomfortable as Bob and to whisper amongst themselves.

"Bob, you're kinda messing up the hero thing right now. You gotta do something," Ned whispered.

"I thought they were gonna kill me like a second ago. What do I do? Haven't had anyone cheer my name ever."

"Yeah, it's part of the territory. Haven't you seen the movies? Just do a movie thing."

"My friend, you are heavy, and you are wet. Can we continue inside?" Sergio said.

"Oh, right. Sorry, Sergio," Bob said. They continued walking to the lobby.

It seemed to have reinvigorated the crowd, who continued their chants and cheers. While Bob couldn't see Charlie, the crowd noticed him trailing behind. Charlie gestured for them to turn down the excitement, which they did.

Once inside, they placed Bob on a couch. The cushions were torn apart, and stuffing puffed out, but nothing else was in as good of shape. The crowd began to gather around an uncomfortable looking Bob. Again, Charlie signed for everyone to look away and be nonchalant.

"I don't get it," Bob whispered. "How did you convince them to stop fighting?"

"They all saw Marie go into the water and Sarah not caring," Charlie said. "Everyone stopped fighting and sprinted to the water, but you beat them to it. They tied up Sarah and Reginald while we grabbed you in the water."

One thug stepped forward while wringing his hands. At first, he wouldn't look Bob in the eyes, but looked up after a couple of moments. "Yeah, a lot of us were just in it for the pay. Tammy over there is just a high school intern. They took it too far when you mess with kids."

Sergio appeared from behind the check-in counter with a blanket and some Still Rivers gear: yacht club shirt, hoodie, and sweatpants.

"You really are a crazy man, Bob," he said. "But I am so grateful. You saved my—*our* stores. You are a hero." All the owners and chefs nodded, some verbally agreeing.

Bob smiled, but it was short lived. His brain was working again, and he remembered his parents were gone.

He frowned, and his body slumped. His audience reacted the same way.

"I'm not cut out to be a hero," Bob said. Everyone stayed quiet. He headed to the bathroom to change into the clothes Sergio brought him.

After changing in the stall, Bob stared at himself in the mirror. He looked at each of the cuts and bruises. His eyes turned toward his injured shoulder, which looked slightly swollen. He couldn't do this every day. Bob knew Lila would support him, but he'd have to hide it from his parents. However, he was a terrible liar. Not only would he have to lie to them, but he'd also have to lie to his boss, Emrys. Then he'd have to lie to any "villains" they encountered. Bob kept his identity a secret for less than a week, also revealing Ned and Charlie. There was no way he could keep it a secret, and again, everyone he loved would be in danger. Then his mind turned to the worst part.

The attention. An entire city of people would cheer him on. Millions of people would know his name. Some might even dress up and pretend to be him. Bob was uncomfortable with a lobby full of strangers. What if someone called out to him, and Bob didn't know the person's name? Would he be honest and say some generic term of endearment like buddy or pal? That could work for a stranger, but what if he met the person before? How many times could he pretend to know someone's name?

"Bob! You okay in there?" Charlie called out from the lobby.

Bob snapped out of his mental spiraling, unfortunately knocking over a ceramic soap dish on the bathroom counter. The dish slid off the counter and crashed onto the floor.

"Yeah! Be out in a minute!"

He washed his face to wipe away any of his mental

anguish. Bob couldn't do this again. He was happy to try it, and if they really needed him, he would help. This wasn't how he wanted to spend his nights and weekends. His stomach tightened, but he knew it was the right choice.

Bob returned to the lobby. He plopped onto the couch with a defeated look on his face.

"A shame Chicky Chicky Parm Parm didn't survive the battle," he said, gesturing to the sopping wet costume in his hands.

"A real shame," Ned said.

Charlie nodded. After he and Ned changed back into civilian clothes, Charlie gestured with his head for the three of them to step outside. The bitter wind chilled Bob but not as much in dry clothes and a new, dry blanket. They walked solemnly to the edge of the dock, next to Reginald's yacht. Bob tossed the mask into the water. Before he threw the rest in, Ned placed a hand on Bob's non-injured shoulder.

"I'll hold onto the rest. This is really expensive stuff."

Bob worriedly stared at the mask.

"You don't have to jump in after it. It's fine. The rest of it was the expensive part."

"Oh, thank God."

After passing along the rest of his costume, Bob and his friends silently stared out into the night. After a few moments, Ned mournfully spoke.

"I'm sorry, Bob. I loved your parents. Maybe they're locked up somewhere and okay. We can find them."

"I appreciate it, but I can't lie to myself." Bob gulped. He felt his tears swelling and chest tightening. "They got here before your parents, and no one's seen them since."

Charlie rested a hand on Bob's shoulder. It looked like he wanted to say something, but he didn't. The three stared out into the water and watched the mask drift off in the distance and vanish. Bob then looked over at his parent's boat.

"Why are the lights on?" he said.

"What?" Ned said.

"My parents' boat. The lights are on," Bob said. There was joy in his voice. "Their lights are on!" He trotted over, which was the fastest he could go without being in pain.

"Wait! It could be a trap," Charlie said.

Bob didn't care. He kept going, and the two superheroes trailed behind him. He climbed onto the back of the boat and shouted. "Mom! Dad!" he said. There was some ruffling inside the boat and whispers.

"Bob?" his mom said. She sounded surprised. "Is that you out there?"

"Yeah, Mom. It's me." Bob said, his voice sniffly. He got closer but stopped when his mom shouted.

"Wait! You...Just stay right there. Give us a second," she said.

Bob blushed when his parents walked out from the yacht's cabin. Their hair was messy, outfits were lopsided, and their own cheeks were red. His mom adjusted her dress as his dad slipped a belt into the pant loops.

"What's, uh, wrong, uh, champ?" his dad said.

"Bob!" his mom said and ran to him. "What happened to your face? Oh, my!" She inspected his face and examined his shoulder. "Whoever did this to you is gonna get it ten times worse. You never mess with a momma's cub. Greg! Get the damn keys. Bob, tell me who did this to you. Tell me!"

Bob hugged her, tears streaming down his face. "I'm okay."

"Why are you crying? Oh honey," she said. His dad joined in the hug.

"Bob, you know your mom is gonna ask until you tell her," he said.

Bob nodded. He didn't care about anything outside of this hug. It was then that Ned whispered to Charlie.

"We don't need to be here for this."

"Yeah," Charlie said, then cleared his voice. "Hey, Bob, let's wait back by the lobby."

Bob's mom excitedly nodded. "That is a wonderful idea. You let your dad and I finish up in here, then we'll meet you guys."

Bob frowned. After mourning, he didn't want to give up any time with his parents. If he kept them in his sight, he could keep them safe.

"Do you need help? I look hurt, but I can stick around."

"Oh, no, no, no, no," his dad said. "We are alright, Bob."

"But I—"

Bob suddenly felt Charlie grab a hold of his non-injured shoulder. He whispered to Bob.

"Take the damn hint, Bob."

Bob felt the vomit rise in his throat, but he successfully held it back. It was like all the circuits connected as he reexamined how his parents were dressed. His parents were always fashionably impeccable at the club, but now they dressed like a couple of people who quickly threw on outfits in the dark. Bob almost vomited again but raised a thumbs up and left with Ned and Charlie back to the club. It didn't help that his parents giggled like school children as they retreated into the cabin.

Bob took a seat at a table on the Still Rivers' deck. Charlie and Ned sat as well. Ned smiled and snickered at Bob.

"You're not really observant, are you."

"You know what? I thought they were dead. Sorry for not picking up context clues!"

Charlie poorly stifled a laugh but just smiled at the two of them. As he turned his gaze back to the water, avoiding the side of the docks where Bob's parents were, he sighed. "What a day."

About ten minutes later, Bob's parents returned, and Sergio walked out on to the deck.

"Excuse me," he said. "Reginald and Sarah cannot join but told us to serve you."

Bob raised an eyebrow, but Sergio gave him a wink.

They headed up the deck stairs to the banquet hall.

All the tables were still shoved up against the wall, except for the one table in the center. It was set and adorned with candles. The lights were dimmed, and one of Reginald's thugs played a harp in the far corner. A few of the clerks stood by the table, white cloths draped over their forearms, the other arm behind their backs.

The Loroxes sat at the table, wine in hand, and turned to the Johnsons with glasses raised.

"Good to see you Greg, Abby!" Mr. Lorox said. "Come on over!" He started pouring them wine.

After everyone sat, the clerks took their orders and served appetizer after appetizer. There were dozens of chefs that Bob didn't recognize, but they spoke to him like they knew each other forever. He enjoyed everything they served, though he was wildly uncomfortable with the small talk. Someone was missing, though. Then he appeared.

Sergio stepped into the banquet hall carrying a plate of chicken parmesan, steam wisping off the top. Bob's mouth started watering. He smelled it. The thing he had fought long and hard for.

It was the most delicious chicken parmesan he ever had.

He savored every herb, every spice, every tomato chunk. He savored the fresh mozzarella melting over the top. He savored the perfect, crunchy, and well-seasoned crust. They played a flavorful symphony in his mouth. Then there was the sauce that whispered to him like a savory muse. It brought back every childhood memory, the good and the bad. His grandpa made it to celebrate Bob getting his first job out of college. His mom had made it to cheer him up the first time he was dumped. It was the first meal he made for Lila. The very same meal that started him on this crusade.

Bob looked around at everyone, happy and laughing. It was just like things were back in the day. Bob suddenly felt like a kid again with his friends over for dinner. He and Ned had just finished soccer practice, band practice or whatever activity they were doing at the time. Charlie showed up with some cool story or some fun thing to do after dinner that got them all excited. Their parents smiled and laughed with each other about what was going on in their lives.

That was the beauty of food. Some people made food transactional, which was fine. Food served a purpose. Sometimes a person just wants a cheap snack or just wants to stretch a paycheck to feed himself. But food was also an act of care and appreciation. Cooking to bring friends and family together. Cooking to get over a loss or a hurt. Cooking to remember someone who isn't around anymore or a tradition that you want someone else to experience. He definitely tasted all the love and appreciation in what he ate tonight. After finishing his last bite, Bob leaned back and smiled.

"You gonna be okay there, Bob?" Mr. Lorox said, gently patting him on the back. "I think you had more chicken than I'll eat in a year."

Bob chuckled. He looked down at his clean plate and smiled. Sergio had given him at least four servings, but he stopped counting after that. Each time he finished his plate, another just appeared. It was delicious. "What do you mean? I never got served."

"Oh, Bob. Stop it. You're gonna give yourself a heart attack from all that eating!" Bob's mom chimed in. Sergio peered out from behind the swinging doors that lead to the kitchen, but his mom gave him a dirty look. "No more! No man should eat this much chicken!"

Sergio's laugh echoed behind the door, and he called out. "Okay, okay. I go. I see you on Monday, Bob!"

His mom turned to Bob and grabbed onto his forearm. "You are not to eat any more chicken, young man. That was horrifying. You have to wait at least two weeks."

"I'll be fine, Mom. It was just so good. I couldn't stop." Bob leaned back in his chair and lowered the waistband of his borrowed sweatpants, allowing his gut to peer over the top a little more. Unfortunately, as he relaxed, he winced. His shoulder was still in bad shape.

"You alright there, Bob?" Ned said from across the table. "Maybe we should get you to a doctor. Reginald did a nasty number on your shoulder."

"Yeah, Ned's right. Mr. and Mrs. Johnson, do you mind if we take your son? Then, I promise it's straight to bed with him."

Bob's mom snapped her gaze to Ned, with a mechanical efficiency. Her head slightly tilted, and her eyes flared. For a moment, Bob thought they were going to catch fire.

"Ned, honey, did you say Reginald?"

"Um...No."

Bob stuttered and said, "Yeah, he said...Ronald."

"Robert Andrew Johnson, don't you dare lie to me. Now, did Reginald do this to you?"

"Yes..."

His mom was quiet, but everyone at the table looked at her horrified. They were an audience waiting for something tragic to befall an unsuspecting person. Even the chefs, thugs, and clerks seemed to have gone quiet downstairs. She finally spoke in a tone more haunting than anything Bob had ever heard before.

"I swear to God, when I find that man—"

"You'll hire an attorney," his dad said. "We aren't going to be vigilantes, Abby. That's reckless, irresponsible and a bad example."

"Oh, no. You hurt my son. I take justice into my own hands. It'll be a great example. The perfect example of what happens when you fuck with my son."

His mom continued, "You guys take Bob. Get him patched up. Best of *everything* they have there. Ocean view room. I don't give a damn. Tomorrow, I'm ruining that man's life. Fuck this club. By the time I'm done with coconut head, I'll own this damn place." Bob's mom slammed a napkin to the table and stormed out of the banquet hall, with Bob's dad calling out to her and following closely behind.

Once everyone else felt safe to talk again, Mrs. Lorox tossed Charlie the keys. She said, "You can take our car, Charlie. We'll ride back with the Johnsons and figure out how to ruin Reginald and Sarah. See you both on Saturday. 4:00. Sharp! Grandma is making shakshuka."

Before leaving, Bob thanked everyone in the kitchen again as they cleaned up what they used and packed up what they brought from their own stores. The kitchen was filled with chefs, cooks, and Reginald's former thugs, all chatting away or bopping to the music blaring from a nearby radio. They thanked him back, and Bob headed outside to catch up with Charlie and Ned.

By the time he caught up, Charlie was impatiently sitting in the driver's seat, and Ned was passed out in the back seat, his mouth open and drool sliding down his jaw.

"Hey, Bob. Anyone else you want to talk to? I love waiting. I definitely don't want to get to bed." Charlie angrily tapped on the top of the steering wheel.

"Consider it payback for making me vomit, asshole."

"Bob...Did you just talk back to me?"

Bob smiled. "I guess I did."

"If I wasn't so damn proud of you, I'd kick your ass. Go tell that boss of yours about what happened today. That manager job is yours."

Bob and Charlie chatted for a bit, but the conversation died off shortly after that. Bob rested his head along the window and struggled to keep his eyes open. Occasionally, Ned would snort in his sleep and jolt Bob awake. It didn't work too well, though.

It was a pleasant drive. The full moon painted the world in a faint white and highlighted the sloshing river that separated where they were from Central City. Central City's lights shone like an unwavering beacon. Bob chuckled. After such a crazy night, it was strange almost no one would know about it. Millions of people would go about their days, never knowing that they were days away from losing culinary traditions. He glanced over at Charlie then at Ned in the back seat.

They would never get credit or acknowledgement for what they did. It wasn't fair. He quietly sighed and stared back out the window.

Two bright lights appeared over the hill behind them. It was the first car they had seen since they left Still Rivers.

"Asshole has his high beams on," Charlie said. He snarled and squinted, trying to reduce the impact.

The lights grew brighter as the car got closer. Charlie stuck his arm out the window and waved for the car behind them to go around.

Crash! The vehicle slammed into the rear. Charlie struggled to stabilize the car as it swerved left and right. Since he only had one hand on the wheel at the moment of impact, he failed miserably. Ned snapped awake and screamed.

"What the hell?" he said, staring backward. Bob did the same.

It was a van, double the size of Loroxes' car. It was banged up and painted light blue.

"Stupid car can't go any faster!" Charlie said.

Bob recognized the driver first before he remembered who the van belonged to.

"It's Sarah! She got free!" Ned said. He scrambled to pull his gear out of his backpack resting on the floor in front of him. The back seat was small and equipping himself was going to take too much time. Charlie focused on stabilizing the vehicle. It was up to Bob.

Crash! The van plowed into their car again. Bob twisted too quickly and was in sudden and sharp pain, almost as if his shoulder was slipping out of its socket. He howled.

Charlie roared, "Bob, careful with your shoulder! Ned, I need you to—"

Crash! Whoomp!

Time stopped. Bob felt weightless. His stomach rose into his throat. Something popped, sounding like a quickly filled balloon. A white bag smashed into his face, and blood rushed to his head. His seatbelt pressed against his throat. He couldn't breathe. His head bashed against the window. He was upside down. He was suddenly right side up.

Crunch! The car's frame collapsed as it slammed back into the earth. Then again as it rolled over. After rolling several times, the car groaned to a stop as the momentum was no longer strong enough to keep it rolling. It plopped into a newly formed crater beside the riverbank.

Bob coughed, flecks of blood covering the deployed airbag in front of his face. He watched the flecks of blood launch upward as if they rebelled against gravity. After blinking and feeling the blood swell to his face, he realized they were all upside down, held up only by their seatbelts.

"Ned." He coughed. "Charlie." He coughed. His friends were motionless. Fear gripped his throat, so only a faint whisper came out. Maybe if he said it quietly, it wouldn't be true. "Ned. Charlie." They didn't budge. He tried to reach for them, but his injured shoulder didn't move. He pushed with all his strength, but he couldn't even make it wiggle. He strained to undo his seatbelt with his good arm.

Bob crashed down, landing on his head. He rolled to his stomach and reached for Charlie. His body collapsed, unable to hold itself up.

There were footsteps. They grew louder as the person got closer.

"Help!" Bob yelled, coughing all the more violently from the throat strain.

The footsteps stopped. The person laughed. Bob rolled onto his back right as the person came into view.

It was Sarah. She no longer was the pristine, sophisticated person Bob saw at his parents' induction ceremony or even tonight at the club. Her red hair was tied in a bun. She wore a blue one piece with the sleeves poorly cut off, an orange zipper going down the middle and two orange lipped pockets on either side. Her heavy, black combat boots smushed the car fragments into the dirt beneath her.

She squatted down and stared at Bob. After a huff, she smiled like a wolf who backed a rabbit into a corner.

"You're coming with me." She seized Bob by the ankle and dragged him to the van with strength Bob didn't expect from her slimmer frame. He kicked and screamed, but he couldn't break free. Sarah's herculean grip combined with Bob's exhaustion made him nothing more than a ragdoll.

"Ned! Charlie! Get up! Please be okay!" He turned to Sarah. "Please call 911. They need help."

She silently heaved Bob into the back of the van. He couldn't fight back. There was no energy left in him. His shoulder was busted, he was coughing up blood, and his throat was so bruised, it hurt to breathe. He was trapped.

Chapter Thirteen

Ned's eyes fluttered open. After realizing he was hanging upside down, he released his seatbelt and landed on the ground with a thud. He wiped some glass shards and blood from his skin and took a deep breath. Bob was gone. He might've gone out for help. Charlie remained in the driver's seat, unconscious.

"Bob?" he said. He repeated it a couple times and peaked outside. There were drag marks. He could've crawled to get help. Then, memories slowly returned, and he shuddered at the memory of Sarah's murderous look as she rammed them. Her eyes pierced his soul when they made eye contact before the crash. She made them crash. She was after them. She took Bob and left them to rot. His heart raced.

"Charlie," he said, shaking his brother. After a few shakes, Charlie startled awake, seized the wheel, and panicked. Ned yelled louder. "Charlie—focus! We already crashed. No point in holding onto the wheel."

Charlie slowly let his hands drop down. After freeing

and lowering himself to the car's upside down ceiling, he had a terrified look in his eye. "Where's Bob?"

"She took him."

"Fuck!" He punched the steering wheel repeatedly. "This stupid car! This stupid city!"

"Charlie! Stop being a child! My god! Enough already. Bob needs us."

"Piss off. You don't get it. I got careless, and it ruined everything. This should be a walk in the park taking down Reginald and Sarah, but nope. I messed up. All I wanted to do was do better. I joined C.L.E.A.N., and then I betrayed them. I took over D.I.R.T. and got my ass kicked. I try to save the city and put a crosshair on our family and Bob."

"Charlie..."

Ned thought back to when his brother first got hired to work at C.L.E.A.N., a secret government agency dedicated to fighting global crime and the dirtiest and most violent terrorists in the world. Charlie was so proud and rode his pride to the top of the agent ladder. Unfortunately, he got cocky, and his pride led to him hating to listen to other people. So, he left and took over D.I.R.T., a terrorist organization which stood for everything he spent years fighting. He was going to show C.L.E.A.N. why he did not need to listen to anyone, why no one knew better than him.

For Ned, he just joined because he needed a job, and what's better than nepotism for getting one? Charlie hired him as a security guard. Though he didn't like the job, he did it, and he wasn't bad at it. He had been doing it for almost a year when Bob showed up and took down D.I.R.T. He chuckled, remembering that Bob thought he was filming a show the entire time, never realizing he had become an agent. Without even knowing, he saved Ned and Charlie, reminding them that they should be better. Now, he was kidnapped and in danger.

Charlie shoved his door open and helped Ned out of the back seat. "Things were so much easier back then. Now, all I do is mess up. All I do is make the wrong choice. I thought we were safe. I thought you, Bob, Mom, Dad, everyone—"

"Charlie! Enough with the pity party, alright? You mess up. Everyone messes up. I don't know why I have to explain this to my older brother. If you break something, fix it. If you hurt someone, apologize. If someone kidnaps your friend, go save him."

"Oh, aren't you so smart?"

Charlie shoved him. Ned huffed and shoved back. Charlie returned it. Ned did the same then snorted.

"You know what?" he said. "You've always been like this. A hot-headed spoiled brat. You are the best at every-thing but crack at any mistake. Any failure."

"Oh, that's rich coming from the lazy asshole that spent most of his time in college getting drunk at frat parties?"

"You mean having friends? Having fun?"

"Was it fun when mom begged me to get you a job?"

"I...Screw you, Charlie. Stop being so holier than thou. I remember you complaining to Mom and Dad when Veri-tably didn't nominate you or when Lila kicked your ass. I got drunk, fine. I wasn't great at college, so what? I'm here, right? You and I are at the same exact point in life, except I have friends. You're so goddamn lonely that you decided to dress up in tights and drag me and my friend into your stupid mission."

Charlie trembled with anger, his fists clenching. Ned was equally furious. Adrenaline coursed through his veins and shook his voice. Even his breathing was affected. His lungs and throat felt tight, and his head throbbed.

Finally, Ned continued, "I'm gonna save Bob. Stay here if you want. I don't give a shit." Ned stormed off.

It needed to be said. For all his good qualities, Charlie was still a self-absorbed know-it-all dick. This entire time, Charlie ignored Ned because who could possibly know better than Charlie? Even when they were kids, Ned and Bob would be playing a game, but their game was dumb, and they should do what Charlie wanted. Bob wanted an older brother so badly, he just went along and listened to Charlie like it was God himself talking. Here the cycle was repeating. Again, Charlie had an idea. Charlie wanted to do it with...him. After all, who would have his back better than Ned?

After stomping a few feet away, he stopped and sighed, expelling most of his anger and returning his voice to its gentle, normal state. However, he wasn't ready to turn around yet.

"I've noticed you being reckless. Like when you and I took down that warehouse. You didn't care about what happened to us, just that the result got done. I tried to say my piece, but you didn't care. It hurts, alright. And I didn't mean what I said about you not having friends. I basically just have you and Bob, and Bob is just as much your friend as he is mine."

Charlie didn't respond. Ned turned to find him walking over with a downtrodden look on his face, like a dog that knows he did something wrong.

"Had that in the chamber for a while, huh?"

Ned nodded. Charlie did too.

"I'm sorry," Charlie said. "I can't promise that I'm gonna change because I don't want to let you down again. I just hope you know that I drag you along because I trust you, and no one has my back better than you. It's because I know you're there that I take these risks. No one can beat us together."

Ned wiped a tear from his eye. It was a weak apology by any normal standards. For Charlie, that was as good as it was going to get.

"I'm so fucking tired. It's so late, and I didn't take off work tomorrow."

"Now who's the whiney—"

"Charlie, I swear to—"

"I'm kidding! Let's save Bob, so we can stop playing superheroes."

Ned called a taxi with his phone, though it was tough with a shattered screen. It took about fifteen minutes to arrive, which gave them time to slip back into their superhero costumes. When the taxi arrived, it approached very slowly like it was just idling ahead. Ned couldn't blame the driver since he and Charlie probably looked very strange in their costumes, standing on the side of the road in the middle of the night next to a totaled vehicle. Ned was grateful he didn't just speed past them. The driver stopped the car and cracked his window just enough for his horrified voice to come through.

"Are you...King Grigio?"

"Yeah. Are you Zhang?"

The driver nodded.

"Okay, awesome. Mind popping your trunk? My brother has got to throw some stuff in the back."

The trunk clicked open, and Ned continued.

"Thank you so much. Charlie, make sure the plates match."

Charlie heaved a sack holding his compressed spatula

weapon and various goods into the trunk and the SUV taxi sank a bit. It sank even more when Ned and Charlie got into the back seat. The driver glanced back in the mirror, still visibly afraid.

"So...where too?"

"Sunside Piers." That was the last place they saw Sarah before the club. It was also Raghu Distribution's strongest bastion. Sarah had to have taken Bob there.

The driver opened his mouth to say something, then pursed his lips together and put the car in drive.

"Mom says she got the car, right?" Charlie said quietly.

Ned nodded. Once Zhang started driving, the two took a much-needed power nap.

After an hour, they were still in the car, but Ned felt like he was only asleep for a few minutes. He wiped the drool from his face and appreciated not waking up upside down, something he didn't expect to be grateful for. Ned adjusted himself and peeked outside.

There were hundreds of bright red taillights shining back at them, reflecting off the raindrops that dotted the taxi's various windows. The driver slammed on the horn a couple of times and yelled at another driver through his open window. He was a lot braver in his element.

Drivers on either side fought to make their way to the side streets, which was extremely hard to do in stand still traffic. Ned turned to the driver.

"Did they block off the road?"

"Looks like it. I see some cop lights a few blocks down. Kinda close to where you guys are going."

Ned shimmied forward and poked his head forward. The driver was right. Police had blocked off the street,

Sunside Piers in the distance. There were a dozen officers guiding traffic away or getting ambulances or back up into the zone. The echoes of megaphones projecting orders over each other became almost deafening to people getting closer.

"Charlie," Ned said, shaking his brother awake. "Things look bad."

"What?" he yawned. "Things? Is Bob okay?"

Ned slid back, so Charlie could take his place to look outside.

"Crap. We'll get out here. King, can you pay? I can't reach my wallet." Charlie got out of the car so fast he didn't hear Ned sigh. He quickly paid and thanked the driver.

"We'd also appreciate if you don't mention this ride to anyone. Secret identities and stuff."

"I ain't no snitch." Zhang smirked.

"Have a good night!" Ned said, and he slipped out after his brother.

The police orders were as chaotic as Ned thought they would be. They yelled at various drivers to go in various directions. They told reporters and onlookers to back up and not cross their barricade. They relayed information to each other, which seemed to become outdated seconds later as a new update came across. Ned spotted Charlie weaving through the cars, careful that his armor didn't scratch anyone as he passed. The rain tapped against his costume like rain hitting a tin roof.

Ned shivered, unsure of whether it was from the cold rain soaking his costume or from seeing the city like this. "Hey, Cap, hang on!" He jogged ahead to catch up.

They made it past the honking drivers and to the mob, consisting of at least two hundred people, that gathered outside the barricades. News crews and the onlookers alike recorded the situation unfolding. However, though the reporters demanded answers from the police holding the line and the onlookers merely "oohed" and "awed", Ned couldn't get a good look and muscled his way through, apologizing occasionally for anyone he bumped. Charlie was much more forceful and less apologetic.

Once they were a quarter of the way in, people started moving out of their way and turning the cameras to them.

"Oh, my God, is that them?"

"Who? Wait. It is!"

"Hey, out of the way! The heroes of Central City are here!"

"I saw posts and reels about them!"

"They saved my grandpa's store!"

The whispers quickly grew to cheers and applause as people stepped aside to make a path straight to the barricade for King Grigio and Spatchy Spatch. Ned smirked knowing that it was driving Charlie nuts that people weren't calling him Captain Utensil.

"Go get them, King!"

"Spatchy Spatch! Please save my son!"

Ned was grateful he wore a mask because he was blushing very hard and very moved. He raised a fist in the air and the crowd erupted in excitement and whistles.

"King Grigio and Captain Utensil are here!"

He tried to correct the crowd, but it didn't work. The crowd continued to call Charlie by the wrong superhero name. Ned stayed silent and focused though once he reached the police line, he addressed the highest-ranking officer he saw, who was a redheaded man with a red beard and a stocky build.

"What's the situation, officer? We got an ally harborside, and he's in trouble. We gotta get through."

"Hey look, buddy. I don't care what they're saying. A lot of people got allies in there. Stay behind the line, alright? We can handle this."

Charlie wrapped his fingers around the metal barricade, and Ned could've sworn that he heard the metal creak from the force of Charlie's grip.

Beyond the barricade were dozens of cop cars. Officers took cover behind them with their weapons drawn. There were also officers in swat gear dashing between cars and preparing for an engagement. Ned quickly recognized the hand gestures and formations. They focused on the main Sunside Piers building.

It was a six-story, cream-colored building made of painted bricks with large glass windows and balconies lining every floor. All the outdoor tables and high tops that normally sat outside laid knocked over and strewn about the sidewalks. Some tables were impaled into cracked, but not shattered, windows.

Inside the building were more Raghu thugs, though not all of them wore the traditional biker gear. About a quarter of them wore orange and blue horizontal striped clothes that looked like they escaped from a poorly colored prison. They were yelling at people tied up and huddled on the floor. It was hard to see, but inside was equally a mess. Normally, Sunside Piers was a hub of entertainment, featuring arcades, bars, dance clubs, golf ranges, and anything else you could dream of. Unfortunately, now it was a prison.

On the top of the building, Sarah Crafterson stood ominously, looking down on the city in an outfit that Ned had never seen her wear before. It lacked all the elegance he expected from her. He pointed her out to Charlie, who readdressed the officer.

"Sergeant, let us help handle this. That woman up there

is leading this whole thing, and she wants us. We can end this without innocent people getting hurt."

"Buddy. I appreciate you're trying to help, but this is what we do."

Charlie continued, trying to convince the cop without much success.

Then another officer turned around and jogged over. He had a mop of brown hair and wore a dark leather brown jacket, a flannel shirt underneath and jeans.

"Finnegan, let these guys through. They're the guys that saved Ross's place a few days ago."

"All due respect, Mac, but I'm not sure how some guys in medieval times get ups are gonna help."

"Never doubt the heroes of Central City."

"Fine, but it's your ass when the captain finds out."

A reluctant Officer Finnegan sighed and shoved the barrier so Ned and Charlie could fit through, the crowd's cheers continuing.

"You two better not mess this up. The situation is dangerous," Officer Finnegan said, moving the barrier back into position.

Ned looked up at Sarah, who stared right back at him. She drew something from her pocket, something that looked like a cell phone. She spoke into it then headed into the building and out of sight. Suddenly, her thugs hustled onto the building's balconies, about a handful on each floor.

They hurled white jars at the officers and crowds below.

One cop squinted as the jars came down. She said, "Is that...mayonnaise? I think I recognize the label."

Most people laughed at the thugs' attempt at violence. Then, the laughter turned to screams as the jars made contact. The first one shattered as it hit the hood of a car, and mayonnaise poured out. Then the mayonnaise bubbled and melted through the metal. The next one formed a crater about twenty feet to Ned's left. Another one hit a nearby building and instantly melted away the window and supporting wall, sending a petrifying crack about the city.

Charlie dashed forward onto one of the parked cop cars and leaped into the air. In one smooth motion, he slipped his kneecap bowl off and used it to catch one jar safely.

"King, if they don't crack, there's no reaction!"

Ned reached to the top of his backpack and adjusted some settings. Then he fired at the deluge of mayonnaise jars raining from the sky. However, instead of the normal wine shots, it fired wine jelly that created a gooey membrane around the jars, allowing them to hit the ground without cracking.

"Finnegan! Mac! Get everyone back!" Ned said.

"You heard the man!" Finnegan shouted through his megaphone. "Move your asses!"

Ned and Charlie made their way forward, disarming any mayonnaise jars before they turned acidic. The surrounding officers then scooped up the uncracked jars and moved them out of the area.

"Stop them!" Sarah's voice rang out, even over all the disorder below. She must've come out to see Ned and Charlie fail. More thugs sprinted out of the buildings and started hurling oversized uncooked penne noodles, each about the size of a television remote. They whistled through the air and shattered car windows with ease. Ned trembled at the idea of what they'd do to the officers' body armor. Their gear wasn't nearly as strong as what him and Charlie had.

Charlie slipped his knee cover back into place and unsheathed his spatula. The shards glanced off his armor, and he shattered any pasta that was aimed at an officer. Ned switched his blasters back to liquid mode and shot the projectiles out of the sky.

At this point, they were underneath the awning of the cream building, and thugs rushed out to attack them. Charlie engaged them first. Ned shot at any thugs who got too close but focused on protecting the retreating officers. If any of them got hurt or dropped a jar, they lost, and they weren't losing again tonight.

Officer Finnegan called out over his megaphone. "We got it from here! Go save the city!"

Ned nodded. He and Charlie entered the lion's den.

Chapter Fourteen

Bob coughed himself awake. He couldn't feel his right arm. He tossed his head backwards and looked up at a black, sound proofed ceiling. Things didn't register yet. How did he get here?

He remembered being in the back of a van, being tossed around every time the van turned sharply. Then, some thugs tied him up and brought him here, where someone tied him to a chair. At some point, he fell asleep. He hadn't seen Sarah since she threw him into the van, but she had to be around here somewhere.

The room was round. The right side faced the water, and Bob could see dozens of police boats bobbing in the water. There were biker thugs and thugs wearing orange and blue prison uniforms, all of which were barricading the window with turned over tables and any furniture they could find. The left side of the room was where a semi-circle bar sat, the curve of which extended out into what Bob assumed was the dining area or dance floor. Bob was the only one in the room that wasn't working for Sarah.

He remained silent and just watched what was happening. Then he heard her voice blare through a few hand radios.

"Stop them!" she said.

There were some explosions and popping sounds coming through the hand radios. Then her voice cut out.

Them. It didn't look like the police were moving. The boats remained motionless. Could it be Ned and Charlie? If it was, he had to help. Bob tried to move, but his swollen shoulder sent a paralyzing pain throughout his body. He grunted and one of the thugs noticed him. He was a skinny man with a cockney accent.

"You're awake. Good. Boss was waiting for you to come back."

The skinny thug whistled, and two hulking thugs dragged Bob's chair out at an angle and the two chair legs touching the floor screeched as metal ground against wood. They dragged Bob out of the bar and into an elevator, up to the top floor, down another hallway, then out to a smaller dining area.

It was a square room with glass walls. None of the lights were on. The only illumination came from the surrounding buildings with their own lights. The wooden floors had harsh scratches from people dragging the tables and chairs to the right side of the room and tossing them onto each other.

Sarah stood along a wall, staring out into the city below her. She wore the same outfit though her composure and poise had returned, hands clasped behind her back, chin high.

"Ms. Crafterson," the skinny thug said. "Bob has woken up."

Sarah didn't react for a moment.

"Miss—"

"I heard you. Leave him and go. The shattered body of a former vigilante is of no concern to me. You three have more pressing concerns."

As the thugs quietly retreated, Sarah slowly turned and thoughtlessly tossed something to the floor in front of Bob. It looked like a soggy, red rag with black specks of rotten leaves, bundled up, and it had a musty odor like someone had left it in a washing machine for a bit too long. Bob knew exactly what it was.

"You recognize it? You shouldn't leave things lying around. After I knocked out those idiot cooks that caught me, I escaped along the river and found it caught in some reeds. I couldn't save Reginald, but surely this is a great runner up prize." She walked toward him and stopped once she was about five feet away. Her voice turned into a ferocious whisper.

"I will use it to crush the spirits of anyone who would question me. After all, who would challenge the woman who killed Chicky Chicky Parm Parm? Every store, every bodega, every deli will beg me for orders and mercy. Then, I'll go after the waste-of-space friend of yours that posted the video. Then I believe Lila would be next. Your parents... They're already taken care of."

Bob smirked. Little did Sarah know that his parents were going to rock her world tomorrow.

"What! Why are you smiling? God! How can I hate someone so much? Answer me!"

"Why? You won, right? Can't you let me have something?"

Bob blinked. In the next second, Sarah had a razor-sharp spork pressed to his neck. Her tone turned more sinister as her hot breath sent cold shivers down Bob's spine.

"No. Reginald already offered that to you. You spat on

his generous hand. I'm not as generous. Now, are you ready for your goodbye?"

Without breaking eye contact, she severed the ropes tying Bob to the chair then smirked. "Put it on. It's time to make your final appearance."

* * *

Charlie collapsed against the wall, looking for help to stand. He took fast, shallow breaths as Ned finished the last thug on this floor. Breathing burned like frost down his throat. His brother was in equally rough shape and flopped onto the opposite wall.

After fighting through a horde of thugs, they were on the third floor in a long, mustard yellow wallpaper hallway that connected the various bar rooms.

Charlie tossed his shattered spatula staff to the floor. A thug had taken a tire iron to the center, and after so many blows, it broke mid combat and was no longer helpful. Another thug had ripped the wiring for Ned's wine guns, so he only had white wine on his right hand.

"You. Getting. Tired?" Charlie struggled to say.

"Not even. A little." Ned laughed in between deep breaths.

With a groan, Charlie forced himself to his feet though he kept a hand on the wall for balance.

"This is so much worse than being an agent."

"I was a desk jockey at the damn place. How do you think I feel?"

Charlie, slightly confident in his balance, trudged to the elevator now that he caught some of his breath. Ned trailed quickly behind him.

"Bob, here we come."

Bing. The elevator doors opened.

"Crap," Charlie muttered.

Inside the elevator were about five thugs. Charlie had no idea how they were going to make it to Bob. Before anyone could move, Ned roared and rushed into the elevator with a fist raised. Before joining the fray, Charlie whispered, "Hang in there, Bob."

* * *

"Put it on," Sarah said, pressing the still-wet mask into Bob's hand. She had the decency to move the razor-sharp spork from his neck and place the mask into his non-useless hand. Bob looked around.

There had to be something he could do. There was always something. Unfortunately, the room was bare. There were some tables and chairs pushed up against the wall. Then there was a small drink cart with a half-filled whisky glass. There were other glasses though all of them were empty and clean. Maybe she was impaired from drinking? Maybe that would give him a chance. However, Sarah's breath didn't smell like alcohol, though.

He tried hiding drinking from his parents back in high school enough times to know that a breath mint or mouthwash was just as obvious. Nothing, though. There were no tells. He turned back to Sarah, who looked impatient.

"Do you need help putting a mask on? I understand you went to public school, but they must've at least taught you that?" she said then turned back to look out over the city. "You know I always hated this place? I always thought Reginald and I should move our business to a better part of the country or somewhere warmer. A place like Florida, where you don't have to pay taxes. He never agreed, though. He said it was because there was no place that had as much demand, but I think it was just because he liked it here. He always tried to help it even though you idiots swatted his hand away. We served on councils, ran non-profits, put together fundraisers. Nothing fixed the city."

Bob, half paying attention, struggled to put a mask on with one hand.

"My God! Are you still putting that mask on? How were you able to stop Reginald?" She slipped her razor-sharp spork into a pocket. With a huff, she snatched the mask from Bob. She was distracted! This was his only chance to get away. He just had to—

Thwack! The back of her fist smashed against his face, and Bob toppled to the floor.

"I use the knife next time." She kneeled beside a shocked Bob and forcefully slipped the mask onto his head like a frustrated parent dressing their toddler. "Now, was that so hard?"

She stepped away, and Bob rolled onto his back and stared at the ceiling. At least he had his motion sickness goggles again, not that they were going to help him at all. The smell also didn't help. It was rough in his nostrils when it was a few feet away, and now it was suffocating. He felt like his head was shoved into the gross muck along a polluted river.

"You won't get away with this!"

"Likely not."

"Wait, really?"

"Yes, really. I'm not delusional. I won't be stopped tonight. The police wouldn't dare touch me. You and those other idiots are the only ones who opposed us. Then, with the spirit of this city's culinary world broken, my empire will grow. I'll surrender in a few months with the foundations sturdy. Enough so Nathan can run it while we are gone. I'll serve my time in a cushy jail, as will Reginald. Then we'll be released and enjoy the fruits of our labor."

She might get away with it. Bob gulped. There had to be something he could do. Nothing was in reaching distance, and he couldn't move fast enough to get to anything of use. He knew even with her back turned, Sarah was watching him in the reflection and could hurl that razor sharp spork faster than he could move.

"The real world isn't a game," Sarah said. "A little different from that blockbuster filth you put in theaters. Your enemies will actually harm you here."

If Bob wasn't already terrified, he'd be embarrassed that Sarah recognized him from his TV show turned movie. She glanced at her watch and smirked. Bob saw her face in a glass wall's reflection. She was the predatory wolf he had seen all along. With her eyes narrowed and her fangs barred, Sarah grabbed a chair from along the wall. With two powerful steps, she heaved it into the glass, and it cracked. She swung again.

Crack.

Bob's heart dropped. That was how it was going to happen.

Crack.

His eyes darted around the room. He couldn't sit up. He crawled away.

Crack.

He moved slower than a snail. "Help!" he begged.

"Why run, Bob? I thought you were a hero!" Sarah laughed.

Crack.

"I thought you were brave!" She swung again.

Crack.

"I thought you were going to save the city!"

Clink! The window shattered.

"I guess not."

The shards rained down, falling onto the sidewalks and people surrounding the building. He could hear their shrieks and gasps. A gust of wind rushed into the room like it was coming to see what happened. It was cold and ripped away Bob's hope. Sarah's clothes thrashed about as she stared into the storm of what she caused.

"Are you ready, Chicky Chicky Parm Parm?"

Time slowed down as Bob locked eyes with her. Her pupils danced like wildfire. His breath felt heavy, and his throat tightened. Her hand lashed out. He tried to dodge. She grabbed his collar. He tried to fight back, but she won. He cried out. She dragged him to the shattered window.

Bob stared back at the dark hallway that led toward the elevator. He imagined someone coming out to save him. The person looked like Lila, but Lila was out of town, so it couldn't have been her. The person morphed into Ned then split into Charlie, the shadows of his imagination warping faster than his heartbeat.

The wind grew stronger. He couldn't see where he was going, but it didn't matter. He felt the building's warm air clash with the bitter cold nighttime air. He was getting close to the edge. The temperature was even at first, but he slowly felt his body growing colder and colder like he was passing through to some sort of primordial threshold.

His voice had grown hoarse, and he couldn't yell anymore. His limbs were heavier than what he could move, like someone had strapped hundreds of pounds on each one. Strangely, he laughed. What were the odds that he fell backwards to death twice in one night? Both times he couldn't say bye to Lila. He was at peace, though. Marie was safe. His parents were okay. Ned and Charlie were still fighting. They'd avenge him.

Bob looked back to the hallway shadows that had solidified as two shapes appeared, both wearing weird costumes. One was a barbarian looking guy. The other was a knight.

He heard yelling from down the hallway and out on the streets. It all sounded like gibberish.

Whoosh! The wind slammed into him as if it were trying to pull him outside.

There was only one voice he could understand. Sarah spoke with a cold detachment like someone guaranteed to win.

"Goodbye, Robert."

He fell.

The screams continued from both above him and below him. Sarah looked surprise as she stared toward the hallway. Then a purple spandex covered figure burst from the shattered window and dove toward Bob. The screams from below turned into gasps, and then cheers.

"King! Grigio!"

Bob blinked. He wasn't hallucinating! He reached out his good hand and Ned squeezed it tightly. They continued falling. Ned pulled in Bob and wrapped his legs around Bob's torso.

"This is gonna hurt. Hold on!" he said.

Ned aimed his free hand at the broken window, and a wine corkscrew launched into the metal window frame, a steel rope dragging behind. It sank into the top of the frame with a crunch. The rope grew taught, and they stopped abruptly.

Ned howled as all the stopping force pulled on his hand, wrist, and shoulder. They banged into the side of the building, but it was better than hitting the ground.

"Ned! You okay?" Bob said, his throat sore.

Ned nodded, clearly holding back the pain in his shoulder. He took a deep breath.

"Your legs still work?"

"Yeah," Bob said.

"Okay, we gotta climb. Fast. Charlie is holding her off, but he's not going to last long."

Ned ripped off the last of his wine gun tubing and lassoed Bob's torso. Then they adjusted so both of their feet could dig into the brick mortar gaps as footholds. Bob pressed into his shaking legs and shimmed his hand up the metal rope. Ned used both hands to climb though it was clear he was favoring the one that wasn't just yanked out of its shoulder socket. They covered one story. Then another. Before Bob realized it, they were crawling back into the building.

"No!" Sarah said, fuming. While she was distracted, Charlie charged at her. Sarah rolled out of the way. Before Charlie could react, she slipped the razor-sharp spork into a gap in his armor, and he buckled to the ground. She flipped backwards, swung her leg up, then brought it down with an axe kick. Her heel struck into the back of Charlie's helmet, and he collapsed to the floor.

"Charlie!" Ned rushed forward; his corkscrew claws barred. He swiped twice. The first missed. The second left three gashes in Sarah's outfit across her stomach. Her body was unscathed. She spun to get behind Ned. Sarah whipped out another razor-sharp spork from a pocket. The raised weapon glistened in the light. It was directed at Ned's throat.

Bob roared. He hurled his body forward and fell like a mannequin. He rammed into her and threw her off balance. Her attack barely missed. All of Bob's injuries flared as he smashed into the ground. Ned swung an elbow around and clipped Sarah in the shoulder, sending her onto her back. He followed his attack by hurling his cheese bomb. Sarah flung a leg up and kicked the cheese bomb into the glass wall behind her. The wall shattered instantly from the cheese burst. The cheese web glued together all the shards as they plummet down to the streets.

There was a gasp and a thud from the outside. Bob had to focus. Through the pain, he pushed his body out of the way of the dueling Ned and Sarah. She had gotten to her feet, and now they were trading blows. It was even, though it often looked like she was going to win. Ned was also getting slower. Red began seeping through his costume as new and old wounds opened. Sarah's onslaught continued.

Charlie twitched and sat up. Sarah was too distracted to notice, but Bob did. Unfortunately, Charlie looked like he was concussed from the way his body swayed. Bob gulped. He had to do more.

Sarah was incredibly agile. Her feet moved like lightning across the wooden floors and made her hard to hit. Ned had fired the remaining corkscrew claws on his left hand, but each shot had missed.

Bob's body was barely working and wouldn't be able to help in a fight. He looked over at Charlie, who remained in a daze, and his armor was falling off. That was it!

Bob gestured to his own knee and prayed that Charlie would follow. He pretended to remove his knee protection, which for Charlie was a mixing bowl. Charlie's eyes lit up with recognition. He popped both off and slid them across the floor to Bob, who then slid them behind Sarah. She stepped backwards.

Slip!

She stepped into one bowl, and it slid backwards, taking

her balance along with it. Ned leapt forward and landed a blow right below her collarbone. As she recovered, Charlie's helmet sailed through the air and knocked into Sarah's arm, preventing her from stabilizing. Ned landed another blow.

"You're so annoying!" she said.

Ned swung again. He missed. Right before Sarah could counter, Charlie hurled his spoon-shaped pauldron at her torso, knocking her razor-sharp spork just barely off the path to Ned's throat. Bob tracked her feet and slid the last bowl into her path.

Thud!

Sarah collapsed to the ground. Ned leapt forward and pinned her. She thrashed about.

"Get me something to tie her!" Ned said.

"I'll destroy you! Get off me! Damn it!" Sarah howled.

Bob squirmed to get the wine tubing from his torso and handed it to Charlie, who then crawled over to help Ned. Charlie flopped onto Sarah's right arm while Bob did the same on her left arm. Ned ripped off his mask and smiled.

"It's. Over," he said between gasps. Ned grabbed the wine tubing and tightened it, so Sarah's arms were bound to her sides. She thrashed about for a bit longer, but soon her energy faded. Charlie struggled to stand, but then limped over to the window-impaled corkscrew. He twisted it from the wall and used the slack metal rope to bind Sarah's legs.

Bob smiled. However, with all his cuts and swelling, he wasn't sure how nice it looked. It hurt a lot.

"How about we get me to a hospital now? I'm not okay."

"For sure, Bob," Ned said. "We just gotta do one more thing."

He turned to his brother and nodded. Charlie nodded back. After putting on their masks, they stepped to the edge of the building. Bob watched them look over the city. Their costumes were destroyed, blood seeped from every limb, and they barely stood on shaking legs.

At the same time, Ned and Charlie raised their fists in the air. The city erupted with cheers.

Officers yelled through their megaphones. "Alright, let's get in there! Move! Move!"

Then, the cheers formed into one cohesive voice of the city.

"Spatchy Spatch! Grigio! Spatchy Spatch! Grigio!"

Bob smirked. The city was safe and had two heroes to protect it. The best part was that his friends got recognition.

A few minutes later, Bob heard the police surging out of the elevator. Before they were in sight, Ned snagged Bob's superhero mask and slipped it into the pack. He winked at Bob.

"Enjoy retirement, buddy."

Charlie nodded in agreement. As the cops rounded the corner, Charlie cleared his throat.

"There she is, officers. Also, let's get this civilian some medical assistance."

The cops seized Sarah and dragged her away. She was silent, but Bob knew it wasn't going to be the last time they saw each other. It was like she said before. She'd get out. Reginald would get out. They would try again. That would be a problem for later.

Medics came up afterwards and started dressing Bob's wounds. Afterward, they brought him out on a stretcher and to a hospital. "Spatchy Spatch" and "King Grigio" vanished into the night though the night was far from quiet as the city cheered the names of its new protectors.

* * *

Bob's head sank into the mountain of pillows supporting him. It was the only comfort he had in his hospital room. Everything still hurt, and he couldn't adjust his arm sling. There was a terrible itch that had been teasing him for the past thirty minutes.

Bob looked over at the other patient in the room with him. He was an older guy with salt and pepper hair and a loud voice. He kept yelling at the TV as if the characters were going to hear him.

"Lila! Come on! Get him! You can take that Charlie asshole. My God. This guy! Come on!"

His outbursts were also unpredictable. Bob knew the movie he was watching. After all, it was the one he filmed with Lila, Charlie, and Ned before all this superhero business. The other patient wouldn't react to parts a normal person would react to and his volume fluctuated a lot. At one point, a nurse was sliding a needle into Bob's veins, and the other patient yelled. It startled the nurse, and the needle hurt a lot more than it needed to.

"Hey, buddy!" Bob said, feeling very uncomfortable saying the words and being that loud. He stared into the other patient's eyes. "Can you keep it down? It's a movie!" Bob kept yelling. At a real person. Standing up to someone. A stranger. "They can't hear you, but I sure as hell can." Was this really happening?

The nurse's eyes went wide. Bob started sweating. Beads of sweat drenched his hairline and felt like they were going to burst from every other pore of his body. The man was silent. After a moment, he nodded.

"Sorry, pal. You know how it is. You see, a great movie with a beautiful woman, and you get a little distracted. I'll keep it down, though. Apologies."

Bob slowly faced forward, still failing to believe what

had just happened. In shock, he silently watched his own movie, horrified that he'd have to stand up for himself again. After all, what if the guy called his bluff? Bob couldn't fight him. He couldn't go around punching anyone he didn't agree with.

Before Bob fully spiraled into "what ifs", his nose perked up and his mouth salivated. Ned and Charlie walked into the room. Ned held something sub-shaped and wrapped in tinfoil. The scent was unmistakable. Bob recognized what was inside immediately.

"It's, like, 7 a.m. How did you get a sub?"

"Sergio heard what happened at Sunside Piers and knew you were involved," Charlie said. "This guy tracked us down. Us! Cornered us in a dark alley. Then pressed a hot sandwich into our hands and said 'get it to Bob now or I break your legs'. We didn't have much of a choice."

Ned and Charlie pulled up some chairs and chatted with Bob. Even after some time, the other patient joined in the conversation. His name was Gio. He had just moved to Central City a few weeks ago when he tried some fast-food snails, which were part of the Raghu product line.

"Yeah, it was called *Escargo-to-Go*. Thought it was healthy. Guess I was wrong. Sent me to the hospital. Been eating crap food for a couple of days now."

Bob unwrapped his tinfoil sandwich, which was already cut in half, just like Sergio always cut it. He extended a piece out to Gio, though Ned got up and passed it along since the hospital beds were too far apart.

"No, you don't have to do this. Really? You don't mind?" Gio said.

Bob shook his head. "Please, go ahead. It's a welcome present. This place isn't safe, but it's got good food."

Gio took a bite, and his eyes went wide. Bob knew the

feeling. Everything worked together to provide the ultimate bite. Gio took another bite then another. Each time, the reaction was the same.

"My guy, where did you get this from?"

"Sergio's. Brighton and Tossick. He's got a lot of other stuff, but chicken parm subs are my favorite."

About thirty minutes later, a couple of police officers knocked on the door. Bob recognized them both from his apartment. It was the Wall Street bro and the old guy.

"Dang, it's you again," the Wall Street bro said. "If I see you a third time, I'm arresting you for stalking!"

The older cop swatted him on the back of the head. "Stop being an idiot. This kid doesn't even know you. Can't go around threatening people." He cleared his throat and turned to Ned and Charlie. "Edward and Charles Lorox?"

"Yeah," Ned said.

"We were hoping you could talk to us in the hallway. We have a few questions for you."

Ned bit his lip and turned to his brother, who nodded confidently. The two exited the room.

When they returned, they didn't seem as chipper.

"Good news," Charlie said. "Nurse says you're good to go. Let's get you home."

After saying bye to Gio, Ned and Charlie helped Bob back to his apartment. Bob got Lila's number from Charlie and texted her on a burner phone they bought on the way back to his apartment. The owner had fought alongside them at Still Rivers and refused to charge Bob.

"No! Mr. Chicky Parm? You're crazy. Your money is no good here. Go before I kick your butt."

Bob thanked the owner, and they continued on their journey to Bob's apartment. Once he was safely inside, Ned and Charlie said bye and he laid on his bed.

Hey, it's Bob. Had to get a temp phone. Crazy couple of days. Miss you, he wrote. His phone started ringing immediately. Lila was calling him, and he answered.

"Bob! Green glass door. What?"

Bob smiled. It was the riddle they used to make sure the other was okay. He always had answers prepared.

"Puppies. I'm bringing puppies, leggings, and...shampoo," he said. "I'm okay. I promise. Just a little sore."

"From what? I swear if Charlie—"

"Charlie didn't do anything. I was being dumb. I'll tell you about it when you get back, okay?"

"You are such a pain," she said. Bob heard her giggle from the other side. "I'll text you when I get home, okay?"

"Sounds like a plan. Lo—Good night," he said.

There was a second of silence, then Lila said, "Did you say something?"

"Oh, I...coughed. Good night, Lila. See you soon."

"Oh. Alright. Good night, Bob," she said.

He smiled from the endorphins of talking to her. Bob put his phone on the ground since his nightstand was currently in fragments across the room. He closed his eyes and drifted off to dreamland.

Epilogue

"Why is your arm in a sling?" Lila shouted as Bob strolled toward their meeting spot, only a few minutes late. Her platinum blonde hair was tied back in a messy bun, and she wore the baggy, light blue Pleasant Point Beach sweater she borrowed from his closet and black leggings. She dropped her phone and leapt from the park bench she sat on. Lila dashed straight into a hug, carefully avoiding his sling.

"Oh, my God, Bob. I'm gone for a week—your eye! You're covered in cuts and—is that a bruise?" She inspected him and moved him around like a mannequin. Bob chuckled uneasily.

"I...I was a superhero. Got in a nasty car accident. Then I got kidnapped. Bit off a bit more than I could chew. Speaking of biting, though, I got you a donut. It's from the Fluffy Carousel."

"Our first date..."

She smiled and brought him in for another hug. After gently taking the bag holding the donut, Lila gestured for Bob to take a seat next to her and she started snacking.

They enjoyed one of the randomly nice days in the

early spring. The sun was out. The city's residents jogged down the park's paths, lay about in the grass, and played in the fields. Even squirrels bustled about, looking for their secured hordes for early spring eating. A few birds fluttered between the trees and chirped happily. The best part was that Bob got to spend it with Lila.

"You were a what?"

"Superhero."

"Oh, so I heard you right the first time. Did you hit your head? Wait...The thing you were doing with Charlie."

"Yup."

"You were."

"Yup."

She hugged him again. "I said to be safe. You did such a bad job at it." She laughed. Bob did too.

"I mean, I'm alive, which is the main thing, so I didn't technically totally mess up. I just got some swelling, cracked ribs, messed up shoulder, bruises, and cuts. Nothing that won't heal."

"I'm the action movie star who does her own stunts, but you're the one that's injured. The guy who's working part time at a retail store—a notoriously safe place. Oh, Bob."

She went to rest her head on his shoulder but pulled back last minute. It was probably to avoid hurting him. Bob then watched her decide how to show affection, which ended up with a soft hand on Bob's knee. They then did what they always did together—talk about random things and laugh. Her mind always came up with the most random questions or games.

After getting his fill, Bob checked his watch. The place was almost open. He turned to Lila and smiled. "Let's go for a walk."

They walked over to a coffee cart, grabbed a couple of

coffees, and walked around the city. Bob had a destination in mind and tried to guide Lila without her noticing. Every few turns, he pretended to decide their path randomly. "This way looks fun," he would tease or "I wonder what's over here."

He wasn't entirely convinced she fell for his ruse since he recognized her *I'll-play-along* face. Either way, they kept going and going until they reached Brick Plaza. Occasionally, he did get lost. His mind oscillated between navigating and wondering if everything would go wrong or if she would laugh at him. He was going to say the "L" word today. There were so many ways for this to go wrong. They'd been dating exclusively for a bit, but they didn't see each other super often since Lila was always traveling. Maybe she didn't want anything more. If she did, she would've said *it* first. Was she waiting for him to say *it* first? Or did she just not want to say it? He started sweating, and the present in his jacket suddenly felt like a huge mistake. Bob wondered why it was easier to stare down the mountain Reginald or the wolf Sarah than to say the "L" word to a person he felt that way about. This was such a bad idea.

"Wait! Is this! Bob! This is so cool!" Lila said. She started jumping up and down in excitement. "Bob, did you plan this? Oh, you so did."

As its name suggested, it was a square red brick plaza. Each side was fifty feet. Normally, it was empty, but today was donut day, and lots of local bakers set up in booths around the edges. Lila sprinted to the two greeters at the plaza entrance, one a redheaded, fair-skinned woman with freckles and the other black-haired, tan man. Lila asked for one of the flyers and sprinted back to Bob once she had it.

"Bob! This is such an amazing surprise! I literally want

to eat everything! Crunchy Crema! Magician's Munchkins —Bob, you okay?"

Bob wasn't sure. He said the words over and over in his head, but the idea of saying them out loud terrified him. He stared over Lila's shoulder at the sculpture in the center of the plaza. Four massive, capital letters that spelled out "Love". Each letter was about five feet tall and three feet wide. There were so many couples already there. He had to do it. Just be calm, cool, and collected.

"*I love you!*" Bob blurted, louder than he wanted to, but only loud enough that people within the surrounding ten feet turned around.

Lila smiled and said, "I love you too, Bob." She kissed him on the cheek, and the two continued their stroll. "You were gonna say it on the phone, weren't you?"

Bob smirked.

"I knew it."

"You're too smart, Lila. I can't get anything past you."

Bob took a deep breath and nervously pulled out a long rectangular box from inside his jacket. She looked confused.

"I got you something. I'm sorry for the sweat. I...um... was nervous."

"You got me a present!" She shrieked in excitement and slowly opened the box. "Bob, this is beautiful." She took the sapphire necklace from the box and slipped the silver chain around her neck. After, Lila took out her phone and looked at herself. "How did you match my eyes so perfectly? Thank you!"

"I love you."

"I love you too."

It wasn't scary to say anymore. It was now more like exciting and warming. They grabbed enough donuts to warrant a massive plastic bag and walked out with hands held tightly. They kept walking about the city until they reached News Plaza, a long rectangular cement open space the size of a football field where all the major broadcast stations had their headquarters. Dozens of TVs were set up on the ground floor of the buildings to show current events. But now, they showed the same live event.

"Is that?" Bob said.

Charlie and Ned were on TV, standing next to each other on a stage behind a podium. They were dressed in formal suits. It was strange seeing them wearing regular people clothes. In front of them was a sea of reporters yelling at the two standing alone on the stage. The cameras flashed and clicked.

* * *

"Thank you all for coming," Charlie said. "My brother and I have gotten a lot of questions about what happened to Reginald Raghu and Sarah Crafterson and our involvement with the events at Still Water Yacht Club and Sunside Piers a couple of nights ago."

"Were you present at the club?" a reporter asked.

"Do you know what happened to the masked heroes?" another said.

"What happened to Chicky Chicky Parm Parm—"

"Please. All questions wait till the end," Ned said. After whispering something to his brother, Charlie turned to the reporters. He bit his lip and leaned forward to the microphone.

"We brought you here to say that the rumors are..." Charlie turned to Ned, who nodded. Charlie bit his lip and looked directly into the camera. "The rumors are true." The reporters surged forward, only held back by a line of cops.

"I am King Grigio," Ned said into the microphone.

"And I'm Cap—Spatchy Spatch. Today, we declare that in honor of the fallen hero, Chicky Chicky Parm Parm, we are forming a league. A guild to protect this city's flavors and culinary traditions. If you want to live in a world where people take pride in what they make and not cave into villains forcing flavorless food down our throats, then join us."

A highly decorated cop bolted onto the stage and shoved the two away from the microphone. In a monotonous voice, he leaned forward and said, "I do want to remind those in attendance and those watching from home that being a vigilante is against the law. Please don't put on costumes and beat people up. Call us. We do this for a living. If you want to support businesses, go eat there or get takeout. Do *not* punch food distributors."

Bob watched cops escort Charlie and Ned off the stage. The decorated cop and reporters shouted over each other, turning the broadcast into an inaudible mess.

Bob beamed. He liked the sound of that world, one where all flavors and culinary traditions were protected. But he did his part already. Chicky Chicky Parm Parm was lost during the Sunside Piers rescue. Everyone who saw him without his mask faithfully swore themselves to secrecy. The news broke the morning after that Chicky Chicky Parm Parm's mask was found in the water. There were tributes to him at bodegas everywhere. Sergio, along with dozens of other store owners, spent the day handing out mini chicken parmesan sandwiches in honor of the hero.

"Bob," Lila said. She rubbed his back. "You okay? You kinda zoned out."

"Yeah, I'm good," he said, kissing her on the cheek. Bob pulled his cellphone from his pocket and saw he had a text from his boss, Emrys.

Congrats, Bob. See you at work on Monday for manager testing, the text said.

Bob grinned.

Time for a new adventure.

About the Author

When not writing reports or hanging with friends and loved ones, P.J. Cruz writes books about wannabe actors, wannabe superheroes, and everything in between.

P.J. Cruz has been writing since he was a kid though he took a break during college, during which he earned his Bachelors in Economics and Juris Doctor from the University of Florida. After that, he returned home to the Jersey Shore and writes any chance he gets.

Looking for more?

www.ShoreTerracePublishing.com

instagram.com/ShoreTerracePublishing

amazon.com/author/p.j.cruz

bookbub.com/profile/p-j-cruz

goodreads.com/pj_cruz

Also by P.J Cruz

Bob Becomes an Agent

Bob turns his entire life around to pursue his calling of acting. After attending what he believes to be a filming for a hit new television show, he is accidentally and unknowingly brought into the top-secret world of hygienic espionage. Now while he focuses on the stresses of impressing a potential employer and dealing with his motion sickness, he must act his best to potentially land a big role and save the world from D.I.R.T., Dastardly International Rude Team.

www.ingramcontent.com/pod-product-compliance
Lightning Source LLC
Chambersburg PA
CBHW031651170726
47995CB00015B/740